TRAGON AND THE SCORPION WOMAN

. . . and Other Tales

John M. Whalen

Flying W Press

For Fred Blosser, writer, Robert E. Howard authority, and the man who taught me everything I know about spaghetti westerns.

CONTENTS

INTRODUCTION

The stories in this collection were written between 2006 and 2013 for various online and print magazines. I had a lot of fun writing them, and some of them may be the best things I ever wrote. There were more markets for these kinds of stories back then, than there are now. It was the heyday of a sort of the Neo-Pulp Revolution. The stories are full of energy and fantastic ideas. It is thanks to good people,like editors and publishers Howard Andrew Jones, Johne Cook, Alva J. Rooberts, and Miles Boothe, that these stories got into print.

"Tragon and the Scorpion Woman," first appeared July 2006 in Universe Pathways, a magazine that was published in Greece. It was reprinted by Universe Pathways again in September 2006, this time translated into Greek. That's correct. I can actually boast that Tragon, who eventually became the hero of my sword and sorcery novel, "Tragon of Ramura" made one of his earliest appearances in the language of Homer and Aeschylus. It's a very different take on the Perseus/Medusa myth.

"Island of Fear," was the first story that I actually got paid for. Howard Andrew Jones bought it in 2006 for "Flashing Swords," a nifty little ezine he was editing at the time. It was actually the first public appearance of Tragon and Yusef, two characters that in part were inspired by the old Brothers of the Spear comic that was published in the back pages of the Dell Tarzan comic book. The story's theme concerns the conflict between reason and superstition.

"The King of Sorango," was published in a collection of tales entitled "Shadows and Light," in 2011 by the now defunct Pill Hill

Press. It was Tragon and Yusef's second appearance in print. It has a kind of Robert E. Howard influence.

"The Red Heart of Dolfar," came out in 2013 in an ebook only short story collection published by Heathen Oracle and edited by Christopher Heath. The book was entitled "Azieran Adventures Presents Artifacts and Relics: Extreme Sorcery, An Anthology of Heroic Fantasy." In this one Tragon meets up with a beautiful but slightly insane sorceress with a thing for a certain ruby.

"Bride of the Sea" was published in 2010 by Pill Hill Press in a book called "The Quest for Atlantis: Legends of a Lost Continent." It's the story of the Queen of an advanced, peaceful nation facing down an enemy of superior force in the name of freedom. Written 12 years ago but kind of reminds me what's happening today in Ukraine. Funny how life sometimes imitates art.

". . . Where There Be No Dragons . . ." saw publication in Miles Boothe's Emby Press's short story collection entitled "Blood Trails." A story of a hunter on a hunt for a dragon that destroyed his village and his family. But only he knows the reason why it happened. It's about the hazards of accommodating evil.

"The Hostage of Maldon" is actually one of my favorite stories. It was accepted for publication by a small independent publisher who finally was unable to publish the book. Not the only time that's happened. Haven't really tried to resell it, not knowing many publications that buy short historical fiction without any sword and sorcery elements. Reading it now I'm floored by the medieval dialogue and first person narration, which I rarely use. I almost wonder at times who really wrote this story? Did I channel it?

So there you have it. Eight "lost" stories, five of which feature Tragon of Ramura and his sidekick Yusef Ali Ahmed Nazir. If you want to get into these guys please pick up my novel Tragon of Ramura available from Amazon in print of Kindle.

Thanks to Seth Lemberg and Howard Andrew Jones for helping me recover "Island of Fear." I'd lost my original manuscript but thankfully Seth found the story in the Flashing Swords archive. Also thanks to the good folks at the Internet Speculative Fiction

Database for listing most (but not all) of my published work, which helped me keep the dates of publication straight. Hope you all enjoy this book.

TRAGON AND THE SCORPION WOMAN

1

Tragon of Ramura, Captain of the <u>Orion</u>, dove deeper into the blue water of the lagoon. A beautiful young woman with long blonde hair swam ahead of him. She stopped and floated there facing him. The water was so clear he was able to see her deep green eyes. Then suddenly she twisted her body and dove down toward the bottom of the lagoon. He swam after her as hard as he could, but the girl soon disappeared in the blue hazy depths. He went deeper, searching for her, his lungs aching, his heart pounding in his ears. The girl was nowhere in sight and he suddenly felt panic. Unable to hold his breath any longer, he inhaled and water rushed into his lungs.

"Eurania!" he shouted.

He jumped up in his bunk, his heart hammering, his body drenched in sweat. He gulped deep breaths of air and tried to steady his nerves. How many times had he had that dream? He reached for the goatskin wine sack hanging on a peg in the wall and threw his legs over the side of the bunk. Too many times, he answered himself, as the wine poured down his throat and warmed his stomach. She haunted him. No amount of wine, no other women had been able to extinguish her memory after all this time. He tossed the goatskin down bitterly and got up.

Already dressed in blue linen tunic and ox leather sandals, he stumbled across his cabin and opened the door.

The daylight hurt his eyes as he climbed up the steps and walked onto the deck of the ship. He looked up at the sky and saw dark clouds approaching from the south. They were coming into a storm. The single large sail overhead, with the red Sunburst painted on it, billowed in the wind. He walked to the stern. His first mate Yusef Ali Ahmed Nazir was taking a turn at the helm. The black man from the desert country of Jadia nodded to him, the gold earring dangling from his right ear. A blue loincloth was wrapped around his middle and a sword hung at his side.

"How's our course?" Tragon asked.

"Due South," the mate said. "We should see Ramura in a few days, captain."

Tragon nodded. "I suppose that's good news," he said.

"Aye, captain."

"Under other circumstances, I'd agree," Tragon said. "But as things are, I should turn this ship around and head for anywhere but home. Others have tried that, however. And Caldec made them pay with their lives."

"Aye, captain," the mate said. "His magic has a long reach."

"Someday, Yusef, I'll find a way to— "

Their conversation was interrupted by the holler of one of the men in the bow of the ship.

"Something in the water on the starboard side," he yelled. The men crossed to that side of the ship and peered out over the water. Tragon's eyes looked to where they pointed and saw a small boat drifting aimlessly. There was a man on board. He lay in the bottom of the boat without moving, either dead or unconscious. One sunburnt arm dangled over the side and trailed in the water. Then Tragon noticed something else. A short distance behind the boat, the dorsal fin of a large shark sliced through the water, on a course that ran straight toward the boat

Springing to action, Tragon yanked Yusef's sword from its scabbard and dove over the side. Amidst the shouts of his men, he swam toward the boat as the shark headed straight for the castaway's arm. He got alongside the boat, and suddenly gaping jaws with sharp rows of white teeth, loomed over him. Tragon thrust Yusef's blade into the roof of the fish's mouth, and held it impaled for a second. The creature snapped its jaws shut and nearly took Tragon's hand off.

Without his sword now, Tragon saw the shark bearing down on him. He wouldn't have time to try and climb in the boat. Instead he dove and swam down and under it. The shark bumped the side of the boat and made it bounce and turn in the water. Tragon surfaced on the other side of the craft as the shark circled again. The boat was between him and the Orion. He saw the shark turn. Then it started straight for the boat again, moving fast. The shark's eyes were focused malevolently on him as it cut through the water. Tragon believed it intended to turn the boat over and have both men for dinner. The jaws opened again. And then— pphhhffftt! pphhhffftt!--- two arrows suddenly protruded from the top of the shark's head. The fish reared up out of the water and flailed about insanely. Tragon saw Yusef standing on the deck of the <u>Orion</u> with his long bow in hand. The black man fitted another arrow and let fly. It struck the fish in its belly as it roiled about in the water.

Blood stained the water, and Tragon knew it would soon attract other sharks. He hoisted himself over the side of the boat and climbed aboard, careful not to tip it over. He called for a line and pulled himself to the ship. As the men helped him aboard, he clasped the first mate's arm.

"Once again your skill with the bow has saved my life," he said.

"By the grace of Khemur," Yusef said.

"I owe you and your god Khemur a sword."

"I have another, captain."

The castaway was more dead than alive when they finally laid him on the deck. His clothing was in rags and his body was little more than a skeleton covered with flesh. Yusef knelt down next to the man. He put a ladle of water to the castaway's cracked lips. The man took a small sip. He started to mutter something.

Tragon stooped down to hear what he was saying. The castaway squinted up at him. The pupils in his bloodshot eyes were tiny pinpoints.

"Mora," the man muttered feebly. "Mora. Hideous! Scorpions. Don't look! Don't look!"

"Who are you?" Tragon asked. "Where do you come from?"

"Tried for the treasure." the man said, obviously beyond understanding anything around him. "More gold than a hundred men can carry. But no man can get near it. She guards it too well. All dead from her poison or turned to salt by looking on her face. Every last man."

Yusef looked up at Tragon.

"Of what does he speak?" he asked.

"I've heard tales of a creature," Tragon said. "Half-woman, half-scorpion. She lives in the Ice Country. It is said she has scorpions covering her head and to look on her face turns a man to salt."

Yusef tried to give the castaway more water, but the man suddenly threw his hands up around his head, and began screaming.

"No!" he shrieked. "Get away. Get away!. . . Aaaiiieee!".

The first crack of thunder came out of the now dark sky as the man gave out one last terrible cry and died. The men of the crew stood about, staring down at the emaciated corpse. The wind was beginning to tear at the sails now.

"Make ready to ride out the storm," he told them. He turned to Yusef. "Help me get him down in the hold. We'll give him a proper burial later."

Moments later they were down in the cargo hold and laid the man down on the floor. Tragon patted the pockets of the castaway's tattered trousers. He found a waterproof pouch in one of them. He took it out and opened it. There was a parchment inside. He unfolded it and held it up to the light coming down from the hatchway.

"It's a map," he told Yusef. "A map of the Ice Country and Mora Island. The Scorpion Woman's lair."

He looked down at the dead man, whose face death had frozen into a mask of horror. An idea was forming in Tragon's brain. A very strange idea. One that he wondered if it could possibly succeed or was it simply too insane? An idea that would most likely result in something worse than death.

"He went after gold and found only death." Tragon said. "But his misfortune may turn out to be our salvation."

"We will go after the Scorpion Woman's treasure?" Yusef asked.

"The treasure and something even more valuable," Tragon answered.

2

It was three days after the sighting of the castaway when, beneath a sunset sky streaked with purple and red, Tragon first saw the snowy peaks at the north end of Ramura. A plume of smoke rose from the mouth of the volcano that stood in the center of the mountains. His eye followed the green roof of the jungle that started at the base of the mountains and ran down to the coast and became the verdant backdrop for the alabaster towers and turrets of the city. It was a sight that never failed to move him. But as they got nearer, his mood changed. He saw sheer granite cliffs that rose a hundred feet high out of the water— the Rocks of Sacrifice. He'd seen terrible things done on those cliffs.

"One day I will end up on those rocks," Tragon said to his first mate. "Caldec has me high on his list of suspected enemies. He itches to give his Protector, Belthorian, the order to take me there, tear me apart, and throw what's left into the sea."

"If Caldec ever gives such an order, I will make sure both he and his giant Belthorian regret it," the Jadian said.

Tragon laughed. The Jadian was the embodiment of fearlessness.

"Brave words, Yusef," Tragon said. "But against such power as Caldec's, even your great strength might be no match. Since the day that evil fiend tore good King Daria's heart out with the mere gesture of a finger, he's ruled Ramura with terror and blood. Now he plans an invasion of Xilesia. I believe he wants to spread his evil to all the lands to the west. He will bring Ramura to its destruction, if he isn't stopped soon."

"Who can stop such evil?"

"I've been thinking, Yusef," Tragon said. "Finding that castaway and the map to Mora Island could be the answer to our prayers. A way to defeat Caldec."

"You may find the Scorpion Woman's treasure," the Jadian said. "But what good is gold against magic?"

"Not the gold, Yusef," Tragon said, his eyes suddenly ablaze with the idea that had come to him when they'd pulled the man out of the water. "It is said the only way to defeat someone who has magic is to acquire more powerful magic of your own. The legend says that even when removed from her body, the Scorpion Woman's head has the power to turn a man into a pillar of salt. With the map, we could journey to the Ice Country and take the monster's head. Armed with such a weapon, we could defeat Caldec. His magic would be useless."

"Would such a thing be possible?"

"Only that which has never been tried is impossible, Yusef," Tragon said. "I will think of a way. But first we must deliver this shipment of grain and _talok_ for the lamps and lanterns of Ramura. We must provoke no suspicion of our plans. So far I have been able to convince Caldec that as a Captain in the Ramuran Navy I have bowed to his power and accepted his rule over Ramura. But he seems to have a way of knowing when someone is even thinking of betraying him. We must proceed with caution. I have an audience with him in the morning. I'll secure the _Orion_ a new assignment. A new voyage. But wherever he orders us, our real destination with be the Ice Country."

"Aye, captain," Yusef said. "And may Khemur be with us."

As they sailed into home port Tragon's mind swirled with ideas and half-formed plans of how he might accomplish the dangerous deeds he'd described to his first mate. Then as the ship drifted into the harbor, and the deep purple sunset sky turned the white towers of the city lavender, a strange thing happened. A gull cried out somewhere over the water and for a moment he thought it sounded like a woman's voice calling his name. He stopped and listened intently. Eurania? She called him often in his dreams, but it was the first time she had called him while awake. He waited to hear her voice again but the next time it was only the sound of a gull.

3

It was night when they finally docked. No sooner had they tied the Orion to her moorings, when Tragon saw a squadron of Caldec's elite palace guard march onto the pier and approach the ship. The crew grabbed their weapons. A visit from the guard meant only trouble. Demetrius, a warrior from Golavia, drew his sword and tried to stop them from boarding.

"Stand back," the first guard in the advancing column shouted. Their swords clashed and Demetrius fell to the ship's deck, wounded in the side.

"Hold fast," Tragon shouted at the men. "Let's see what they want."

Ten armed soldiers came aboard. At their rear strode a huge giant of a man. He stood nearly seven feet tall. He wore a bronze helmet and had a sword strapped to his waist. A long black beard fell from his chin and half-covered his bronze breast plate. It was Belthorian, the King's Protector. The soldiers surrounded Tragon and Yusef and drew their swords. Belthorian strode up to them.

"Have you come to escort us to Caldec's palace, Belthorian?" Tragon asked.

"You are under arrest," the giant said.

"On what charge?" Tragon asked.

"You will find out soon enough. Lay down your weapons."

Tragon looked the scene over. They could make a fight of it, but there would be lives lost.

"What of my men?" he asked.

"I have orders only to bring you and the Jadian," the giant said.

"Very well," Tragon said. He drew his sword from its scabbard and dropped it on the deck. He nodded to Yusef, who did the same.

"Stand back, men," Tragon said to the crew. "This is not your fight. Go to your homes and hug your loved ones. We will sail again together soon. Have no fear of that."

"Let's go," Belthorian ordered.

They disembarked the <u>Orion.</u> Tragon marched alongside Yusef between the two columns of soldiers and they headed for Caldec's palace. The walls of the edifice looked blue in the moonlight as they approached IT. The front entrance was through a gate placed between four Dorian columns carved out of marble. After they passed through the gate, Belthorian brought the party to a halt.

"Restrain them," he ordered. One of the guards stepped forward with shackles in his hand. Tragon's fist swung and the soldier fell to the ground. Yusef crouched, ready for a fight, but the guards drew their swords and closed around them.

"Don't try to resist," Belthorian said.

"You're clever, Belthorian," Tragon said. "You knew better than to try this on the <u>Orion</u>. My men would have cut you to ribbons."

"Will you submit, or will you give me the pleasure of killing you now?" Belthorian asked.

The guard Tragon had felled again came forward with the shackles. Tragon extended his arms and the guard fastened them around his wrist. He tightened them as tight as he could, and gave Tragon a sadistic smile. Yusef was similarly restrained. They were marched through the main hall of the palace and into Caldec's throne room. It was a large room with murals on the walls depicting scenes of battles on land and sea that had been fought during Ramura's long history. Torches hung in gold stanchions fastened to the walls. They came to a stop on the red carpet at the bottom of the steps leading up to the throne. The sorcerer-king sat on a jewel-encrusted throne of gold, looking down on them with cold, piercing eyes. He was a thin man with a dark beard that came to a sharp point. He sat hunched forward, his elbows resting on two golden lions carved into the arms of his chair. Long bony hands extended out of the sleeves of the black robe he wore. His fingertips formed a tent and tapped together tentatively as he studied them. Belthorian took his place next to the throne.

"I will dispense with the formalities, Captain Tragon," Caldec said. "You and your mate are charged with treason, the penalty for which is death on the Rocks of Sacrifice. I have brought you both here to give you a chance to escape that sentence."

"Treason's a serious charge," Tragon said. "I hope you can prove it."

"Don't play games with me," the sorceror said. "You have a map to Mora Island and plan to use it in a plot against me. Turn it over or forfeit your lives."

Tragon was stunned. How did he know?

"You can have no secrets from me, captain," Caldec said. "The full extent of my powers is unknown to you as it is to the other poor mortals who inhabit this primitive rock. I established a mental link with one of your crew members. Never mind which one. What he saw, I saw. Through him I saw you take the castaway on board and obtain his map. I know you've hidden it somewhere on the ship. My man searched for it. But it is well hidden. Now where is it?"

"In a place where you'll never find it," Tragon said.

"We are about to go to war with Xilesia," Caldec said. "The invasion of Xilesia is just the beginning of my plans to conquer all the lands to the West. I will need every weapon I can get. Mora's reputed treasure and her cursed head would be a great aid to my plans. With her head I could paralyze all my enemies. I have been searching for her for many years for other reasons of my own. But she has eluded me. Now, thanks to you, my long search may end. Where is the map?"

"You're mad, Caldec," Tragon said, "if you think I'll help you in any way with your insane schemes."

The wizard/king's lips twisted in a crooked smile.

"I thought that would be your answer. And I have no doubt that even weeks spent in the torture chambers would fail to make you tell me where it is. But why should we stoop to such crude methods? I have a better way."

His eyes shifted to Yusef. He raised a hand and pointed his index finger at the Jadian. Yusef groaned suddenly and fell to his knees in pain, his hands clutching at his chest. The veins in his neck began to protrude grotesquely and his white teeth bared in a grimace of pain, as he gasped for breath.

"Tell me where the map is, Tragon," Caldec said, his eyes still focused intently on the Jadian, "or your friend dies."

"Tell him nothing, captain," Yusef muttered through clenched teeth.

Caldec's eyes glowed now as his finger sent out a red ray toward Yusef's chest. The skin on Yusef's chest begin to bulge. In another moment Caldec would tear his heart from his chest cavity.

"Wait!" Tragon shouted.

"Yes, Captain?" Caldec said with a smirk.

"Stop," Tragon said.

The wizard lowered his hand and Yusef went down on all fours, panting for breath, his body glistening with sweat.

"If I tell you where the map is," Tragon said, "you'll kill us as soon as you get your hands on it. But I'll make a bargain with you. Release us and I'll give you my word that we'll go to the Ice Country and bring back Mora's head and treasure for you."

Caldec laughed.

"I have a better plan," Caldec said. "In exchange for your lives I will let you go to the Ice Country alone, but your friend remains here as my prisoner. When you bring me the treasure and Mora's head, he will go free."

"Don't do it, captain," Yusef said. "You can't put such power in this demon's hands."

"We've no choice, my brother," Tragon said. "Alright, Caldec. Agreed. But when I get back, Yusef Ali Ahmed Nazir had better be alive and well."

"Of course, captain," Caldec said. "But just one more thing. I don't doubt that you will return. But just to make sure that Mora's head remains in the right hands, you will take along a passenger." He glanced over at his body guard. "Prepare for the voyage, Belthorian," Caldec said.

"Yes, your majesty," the bearded giant said looking down at Tragon with a crooked smile.

"On your way, captain," Caldec said. "And see that you don't fail. Your lives depend on it."

Tragon nodded at Yusef. The Jadian was on his feet now.

"I'll be back for you my friend," he said.

"If it is Khemur's will," the Jadian said. "Take care, Captain."

4

It was dawn the next day when the <u>Orion</u> set sail for the Ice Country. The crew had been hastily recalled to duty. Their grumbles about shipping out again so soon were abruptly silenced when they came aboard and saw their captain standing in shackles surrounded by six armed guards. They were even more dismayed when Belthorian came up from below, his giant frame barely fitting through the hatchway. The giant gave a short speech, informing them that they were all conscripted by the King to serve under his command. Tragon was to be navigator. He drew his sword and asked if anyone had any objections.

Tragon looked at the faces of his crew and saw fear and anger. But no one objected. As he looked them over, Tragon wondered which one had betrayed him to Caldec.

They got underway. Tragon told Belthorian he would not reveal where on the ship the map was hidden until they were well out to sea, in case he had any idea of killing him once he got the map and returning to shore for another navigator. Two days out he retrieved the map from a secret compartment in his cabin. When he held the map in his hands, despair mixed with anger as he thought of how his plan to destroy Caldec had been turned upside down. Yet, he thought, there might still be a way.

They journeyed twenty days due north through fair weather before reaching the Ice Country. Then high winds, treacherous seas, and ice storms greeted them. Tragon sailed the <u>Orion</u> through black waters filled with ice floes and howling gales. During the nights, he stayed below in his cabin, polishing the surface of an iron shield he had brought along. He worked on the shield every night until the surface gleamed like a mirror.

"I need my sword," he told Belthorian, one night, as the giant watched him work on the shield.

"You'll be given your sword when we get to Mora's cave," the giant answered.

"Afraid?"

Belthorian grabbed the chains shackled to Tragon's wrists and yanked him to his feet. Tragon's knee rose sharply and the giant bellowed in pain and threw him across the cabin. Tragon bounced off the wall but landed on his feet. With a snarl, he dove at Belthorian and managed to wrap the chain around the big man's neck. He got behind Belthorian and pulled the chain tighter. The King's Protector began choking, but, then, with a grunt, threw all his weight behind him, crushing Tragon against the wall. He pounded him against the wall several more times, until Tragon's fingers let go of the chains and he fell to the floor nearly senseless.

5

That night, while chained to his bunk, Tragon slept fitfully. He'd fallen asleep considering the various ways he would kill

Belthorian when he got the chance. And then, while he slept, amidst all these new troubles, the old dream came again. The same as always. Once more he dove down into the bottomless lagoon searching for the girl with green eyes. And for a moment it was a blessed relief to be in another world, free of sorcerors and men plotting for power. How pleasant it was to swim in the cool, clear blue water, searching for her. Searching for Eurania. He saw her briefly then she swam into the blue distance. Then again the panic. His lungs burst and he jumped awake in a cold sweat as the images of the dream scattered in the darkness.

He sat there gasping for breath. He reached for the wine sack hanging on the wall, forgetting that Belthorian had removed it. That dream. Always that dream. It would haunt him until the day he died. He sat there looking out into the darkness and he remembered. It was a long time ago. A lifetime ago.

He saw himself as a young man. He'd been shipwrecked in the southern Sargasso Sea. He had drifted for days on a piece of driftwood and washed up on some rocks at the edge of an uncharted island. As he clung to the rocks, he heard the sound of music. It was a girl playing a harp and singing. He looked up and saw a pair of beautiful green eyes looking down at him— eyes the color of the sea. He thought he must have died and gone to the afterworld, and then he passed out.

When he awoke he found himself in a cave behind a waterfall. The girl with green eyes cared for him, nursed him back to health. She said her name was Eurania. She said she was of the sea. He didn't know what she meant, but when he looked into her eyes he felt himself drowning. She leaned forward and pressed her lips to his. And his world floated away in an explosion of bubbles.

"You are the first man I have ever kissed," she said. "The first man I have ever loved."

They were together for three moons on that deserted island, and they were the happiest Tragon had ever known. He thought he would never want to leave. But one day he saw a ship out on the horizon. And he knew he must return home. He signaled with a fire. She cried and begged him to put out the fire and stay with her. He told her he had to go back to his home, but he would take her with him.

"I am of the sea," she said. "I cannot live in your world. But if you love me, if you believe, you can become part of my world. We could live here together forever. If you believe."

He thought perhaps she was crazy and when the ship sent a boat for him, he grabbed her to take her back to Ramura by force, if necessary. But she slipped out of his grasp and ran out to the rocks and dove in the water. The last he saw of her was her slender body shooting down into the green depths, her long blonde hair flowing behind her. That was the moment when he knew what he had lost and would never find again. Since that day he'd been sailing on an ocean of regret.

He looked out into the darkness now and listened to the ship's noises as it sailed through the icy night. That dream had troubled his sleep for a long time, but it seemed to be coming more often now. He wondered why. He wished Belthorian had not taken his wine sack.

6

They journeyed several more treacherous days and nights. All the while Tragon kept his eyes on his crew. The guards kept them away from him, but he caught their sympathetic glances when they thought no one was watching them. But one man he caught several times talking secretly to Belthorian. His name was Korab. He was from Peluria, an island to the west of Ramura. When he saw Tragon coming, he abruptly stopped his conversation with the king's body guard and walked away. Tragon was almost certain he was the traitor. He would deal with him in time.

It was the twenty-ninth day of the voyage. Tragon stood on deck, stinging sleet flying into his face. He wrapped a fur cloak tightly around himself and tried to peer through the hail into the gloom ahead. Belthorian stood next to him, similarly garbed. Tragon could see something taking shape ahead— an island of white snow and ice dotted with streaks of black jagged rock. Dark waves littered with chunks of ice pounded against the shoreline.

"Mora Island," he said.

He pulled the <u>Orion</u> as near as possible to the island's icy shore, and lowered a boat. He climbed into it, the shackles still on his wrists, followed by four guards and Belthorian, who carried Tragon's sword and shield. When they came ashore, the sleet had turned to snow. Tragon saw that the terrain they stood on terraced up the side of a mountain. There was a narrow path that led up to the black mouth of a cave.

"That must be her lair," he said.

After an hour of treacherous slogging, they stood before the cave entrance. They lit torches and undid Tragon's shackles.

"Here," Belthorian said, handing him his sword and shield. The light from the torch gleamed on the surface of the highly polished shield. "We go no further. We will wait here until tomorrow morning. If you haven't returned by then we'll leave without you."

He took a leather sack from inside his robe and handed it to Tragon.

"If you succeed, put her head in this. Come back and we will search for her gold together."

Tragon tucked the sack inside his robe and hefted his torch and shield. He'd already strapped the blade around his waist. He glared at Belthorian, grasping the hilt of the sword tightly.

"When this is over," he said.

7

Tragon moved into the interior darkness, leaving Belthorian and the others behind just inside the cave entrance. As he went forward, the cave narrowed and tunneled downward. It descended so steeply at one point, he was barely able to keep from falling. Then there was a sudden turn and the tunnel leveled off and widened out. The flame from his torch now lit the dripping points of stalactites several feet in length hanging down from the ceiling. After a while he found himself in a huge grotto. The ceiling was at least a hundred feet high. The limestone walls picked up the light from his torch, casting the entire cavern in a pale bluish glow, bright enough for him to see the entire expanse of the interior. There in the ghostly blue light he saw something that made his heart shrivel. Standing in the grotto, scattered promiscuously about, were the stone-still forms of men. They were the salty remains of other treasure seekers— Mora's would-be conquerors. Tragon came near one and raised the torch to his face. A bearded man stared back at him, his arms raised as if to protect his eyes. His face was contorted in a grimace of horror.

A strange clicking, hissing sound suddenly echoed. Tragon turned and saw another narrow tunnel on the other side of the grotto. He laid the torch down and scurried toward a large rock that stood next to the entrance to the tunnel. He pressed himself against the wall and held the shield up to the top of the rock. He turned the shield until he could see the inside of the tunnel reflected on its shiny surface. The days he had spent in his cabin polishing it had rendered its surface mirror-like. But he saw nothing.

He waited. He had only a vague formulation of a plan. His first objective was to kill Mora. He wasn't certain he could accomplish that. But even if he succeeded, then what? He was sure Belthorian and the other guards had plans for him that did not include his returning to Ramura. They would be ready for him to counterattack. All he could do, he decided, was to take things one step at a time. And the first step was taking the Scorpion Woman's head.

He heard something. It was the sound of a body sliding and slithering along the tunnel floor—a shuffling sound. But it seemed to be moving away from him. He came out from behind the rock and looked into the pitch black tunnel. He moved forward slowly, feeling along the tunnel wall. He went ten or fifteen feet and came to a turn. He peered around the bend in the wall and saw flickering torchlight up ahead. He slid along the wall as silently as a shadow until he came to another turn and stopped.

He lifted his shield and held it out into the tunnel. In

its reflection, he saw a chamber lit with torches that hung on the walls. There were chests filled with gold and jewels scattered around the room. Spears and shields made of gold hung on the walls. Fine Pelurian carpets covered the cave floor. And there, standing in the middle of it all, with her back to him, was Mora.

He shivered when he saw the scorpions writhing on her head. His eyes traveled down her neck and shoulders, and down her back. For a moment he sensed something familiar about her. His eyes followed the lines of her sensuous hips and shapely legs. He nearly gasped out loud when he saw, protruding from the base of her spine, the long, curving tail of a scorpion. Its stinger was twenty times the size of a normal insect.

She was hideous, but still he could not shake off that vague feeling of familiarity. Then suddenly, as if sensing his presence, she turned. He saw her face reflected on the surface of the shield. Even in the uneven light from the torches he could see those green eyes. Deep green eyes. Eyes the color of the sea! It was not the face of a monster he saw. That he could have endured. It was a face he never expected to see again.

"Eurania!" he cried.

8

The monster turned his way. "Who is there?" a voice as old as time itself demanded.

For a moment a terrible silence filled the cavern.

"Who calls the name of one who is dead?" she said.

"By the gods!" Tragon said. "How can this be?"

Mora gasped. "Tragon?" the Scorpion Woman asked.

He started to jump into the tunnel.

"No!" she said, turning away. "Stay where you are. You cannot look on me."

Tragon dropped back again behind the turn in the tunnel.

"In my travels," he said into the darkness, "I had heard the stories of the Scorpion Woman but never did I dream that Mora and Eurania were the same."

"You have not forgotten me then," the Scorpion Woman said.

"Forgotten? I can never forget you. How did this horror befall you?"

"Through the treachery of an evil man."

"Name him, and he will live only until I find him."

"An evil sorcerer. His name is Caldec."

"Caldec!" Tragon's brain swirled in confusion and shock.

"It was many moons and many seasons after our parting," she said. "I returned to my island of Lashmir. I was very lonely after you left. I hated you. I grew bitter. I wanted vengeance against my fate. I sat out on the rocks and sang my songs of sadness. I lured many sailors to my rocks and sank many ships. I had pity for no one. One day Caldec came to my island. He had the power to resist me. He walked across my rocks and, when he was near enough, he threw a cloud of strange sparkling dust over me. I fell into a sleep and when I awoke, he was gone and I was as you see me now. The gods must have sent Caldec to punish me for my vengeful behavior."

Tragon watched her in the reflection on his shield. He could scarcely believe that one so fair could have endured such a hideous transformation.

"I remained on Lashmir for another year," she continued. "But then I heard that Caldec was coming back to destroy me. Some say he had a dream that someday a man would kill me and take my head as a weapon to destroy him. I fled and came here where he and no one else could find me. But still men try. Is that why you have come, Tragon? Are you the man whom Caldec fears?"

He saw her looking out at him wearily.

"He told me he'd been searching for you for reasons of his own. Now I understand. He rules Ramura with his evil magic. He is holding a friend of mine prisoner. I made a bargain with him — to return with your head in exchange for my friend's life."

The claws and stingers of the scorpions on Mora's head

clicked and writhed at this news. The large stinger in her tail reared up, dripping venom.

"His evil grows," she said.

"He plans to conquer the world. I had hoped to take Mora's head and use it to defeat his black magic. But that can never be now. I could never raise my sword against you."

Mora was silent for a moment, as she pondered his words. Then she spoke with a tone of deep resignation in her voice.

"But you must, Tragon," she said. "You must take my head back to Ramura."

"Do not say it."

"Don't you see? It is the only way you can defeat Caldec and avenge me."

"There must be a way to undo the spell he put on you."

"There is no way. I will be as you see me until I die. A hideous monster surrounded by death. Kill me, Tragon, and know it is the kindest thing you could do. If you love me, kill me. At your hands, I would gladly die."

He gazed at her reflection.

"I see no monster, Eurania" Tragon said. "My eyes see only the beautiful child of the sea, who I was foolish enough to leave behind."

"That child is gone, Tragon," she said. "She died long ago. She died the day you left her."

"You could have come with me," Tragon said.

"But I am of the sea," she replied. "I do not blame you. I could not live in your world. We were doomed from the start."

He remembered how she was and a terrible rage flared up within him — a rage against Caldec, against the gods that allowed such things to happen, against himself. And he knew then what he would have to do.

"Tragon," she said. "Do you remember how I used to sing for you?"

"Yes," he said. "Your songs still haunt me."

"I will sing again for you now," she said. "A song of farewell."

He saw her reach down and pick up a golden lyre. She turned her back to him and held the instrument close to her breast and plucked a delicate cord. She sang the song he'd heard that first day, as he'd washed up on her island. He listened again to her words and heard a bitter irony in them.

"You come from far away,
From a land I've never seen.
Borne on the wind and the tide,
A stranger tall and lean.

As she sang, he lowered the shield to the ground and removed his sword from its scabbard. He stepped into the mouth of the chamber, and felt as though he were entering the gates of Hell.

"Listen to my music,
And hear the ancient cry,
Of a love unforgotten.
A love that can never die."

He stood behind her and raised the sword with both hands on the grip and lifted it back over his right shoulder. He hesitated as rage mingled with despair. His fingers tightened on the grip, the muscles in his arms tensed. And then with an anguished cry he lowered his arms to his sides. He couldn't do it.

At that moment, he heard the sound of a heavy footfall behind him. He turned as Belthorian pushed him aside with one hand. He crashed into the wall, as the giant came up behind Eurania swinging his sword.

"No!" Tragon screamed.

He saw her head fly from her shoulders, saw the lyre drop from her hands, and watched her body topple to the floor. He was on one knee, unable to move, unable to breathe. He knelt there as Belthorian turned to face him.

"Caldec didn't think you would be able to kill her," he said.

"And even if you did, he did not want you to return alive. On your feet, or would you prefer to meet your ancestors on your knees?"

Tragon hardly heard the giant's words. All he could do was stare at the headless body of his long lost love. Then something moved within him. His eyes shifted to Belthorian. Horror was replaced by the return of rage and pure hatred. With an animal-like cry, he sprang to his feet and charged the giant. His steel clanged and sparks flew off Belthorian's blade. He struck again and again. On the fourth, their blades locked.

"I told you I would kill you," he snarled. "And then I'll kill your master."

He pushed Belthorian back. But the giant's blade swooshed through the air and the razor sharp tip caught Tragon on his left arm. Tragon backed away, feeling warm blood run down his arm. Belthorian swung again, a grin now twisting his thick lips. Their swords clanged and Tragon stepped back several steps. He bumped into one of the treasure chests and saw some of the gold dust it contained fall to the floor at his feet. He reached down and grabbed a handful of the dust and threw it in the giant's face. Belthorian's head went back and one hand went up to clear his eyes. Tragon thrust his sword deep into the giant's thorax.

Belthorian stood there motionless for a moment, then Tragon withdrew the sword, and blood spurted from the giant's chest. There was a look of incomprehension in the big man's eyes as he touched the wound with his free hand and looked at the blood on his fingertips. But instead of falling, he roared in anger and, raising his sword, charged at Tragon. The wound would have killed any other man. But it seemed only to have made Belthorian more angry. His sword swung viciously in a furious attack. His onslaught forced Tragon to back away.

With a bellow that could have come from an ox, Belthorian swung and as his sword struck, Tragon's sword broke in half. He tossed it aside and backed further away and then tripped over something behind him. He fell down on his back, half-consciously realizing he'd tripped over Mora's body.

He looked up as Belthorian moved in, his sword raised

high over his head. Tragon scrambled back and his hand touched something. His felt scorpions writhing under his fingers! Mora's head! Without looking at it, he grasped it by the hair and lifted it up to the giant. He saw Belthorian's eyes fill with horror. The giant's blade stopped halfway down its descending arc. His face and neck turned white, and then his hair and beard. Tragon shuddered as he saw the giant turn into a snowy white statue, the look of terror permanently frozen on his huge face.

Tragon lowered Mora's head to the ground and wriggled away from Belthorian's salty effigy. On hands and knees he crawled away and sat in a dark corner of the cave, gasping for breath. He didn't know how long he lay there, wimpering like a beaten dog, looking at the petrified giant standing there over the remains of the headless monster that had once been his great love. He lay there and wondered if he would go mad.

Sometime later, he got to his feet and with eyes averted and blinded by tears, he tenderly put Mora's head into the leather sack Belthorian had given him. He found a golden spade among the treasures in the room and dug a grave. He placed the remains of his beloved in the grave and covered her. Then he stood silently over the humble mound of earth with head bowed and said his farewell.

A while later, he lifted his head, the torchlight lighting the madness in his eyes. He lifted the leather sack containing the head of his beloved.

"I'm coming, Caldec," he muttered.

ISLAND OF FEAR

1

Tragon looked up from the map to his first mate.

"It's not on this one either, Yusef. Shall we give it a name?"

The black man beside him rubbed the back of his neck with one hand. The gold earring in his right ear gleamed in the sunlight. "I don't know, captain. Does it matter? Are names that important?"

The uncharted island lay half a league off the starboard bow. A volcano rose beyond its lush jungle, a wisp of white smoke trailing into the clear blue sky. They had sailed westward many days. Tragon knew the island lay not far from the central coast of the Land of Dark People. The arid desert country that was his first mate's native land lay many more days to the north. Here the air was hot and humid. Tragon's skin felt sticky, and his tunic clung wetly to his back and shoulders.

"Names are important, Yusef," Tragon said. "When you name something, it's no longer part of the unknown. No longer something to be feared because it's unfamiliar."

"Perhaps," Yusef said. He looked out at the uncharted island and frowned. "I do not like this place. You people of the West give names and words great power. But there are things in this world that can never be named."

Tragon decided to ignore Yusef's remark as part of the

Jadian's superstitious nature. "It seems peaceful enough," he said. "How about calling it —"

He was interrupted by the sudden appearance of someone on the beach at the jungle's edge. It was a young woman. A blue sarong was draped over her cinnamon skin. She turned quickly to look back into the trees, and her movement suggested fear.

From within the jungle came a harsh, echoing rumble that raised the hairs on the back of Tragon's neck. The girl turned and dashed across the sand. Then something immense broke through the trees, bellowing, and appeared on the beach.

Tragon blinked in disbelief. The beast's body resembled that of an armadillo, only this creature was fully thirteen feet in length and five feet in height. It had a long neck and an even longer tail that swished back and forth in tight, vicious arcs. The beast bellowed and lumbered toward the girl.

Tragon yelled down to the rowers. "Double time! Get us in closer!"

His first mate leaned forward over the railing watching the drama being played out on the beach. The girl sprinted, her long black hair flying behind her. She gained distance from the lumbering creature until she tripped over a piece of driftwood and tumbled onto the sand.

"The beast will kill her!" Yusef shouted.

"Row faster, dogs!" Tragon commanded.

Yusef ran to the mast, and snatched a long bow and a quiver of arrows that hung from a peg. He returned to Tragon's side and fitted an arrow to the bow. The girl was struggling to her feet, but the beast was nearly on top of her. Tragon tore his eyes from her to see Yusef stretch the bow. He heard the string strain against the cedar wood, the "tung" as the arrow flew. It struck the creature in its side, piercing the armored hide. The beast let out a terrible shriek and spun to see what had struck it.

The rowers had the *Orion* close to the shore now, and Tragon saw the animal stretch its long neck, grab the arrow in its mouth, and pull it out. Almost immediately, Yusef launched a second shaft that landed close to where the first had struck. Tragon marveled, as he always did, at the black man's skill with the weapon.

The *Orion's* prow ran up on the sandy shore a few yards behind the animal. Yusef jumped over the side and ran toward it, pausing only to fire another arrow. It lodged in the creature's rib cage.

"Callas, Aldar, with me!" Tragon leapt down after his friend, the crewmen following. Yusef ran past the writhing animal and turned at a point halfway between it and the girl. The enraged creature bellowed once more and charged. Tragon felt sure it would trample his first mate. But Yusef stood his ground and fired another arrow, this one into the center of the beast's forehead. The creature froze in mid-step, blood gushing from its skull. It teetered slightly and then, with a final shriek, collapsed and lay still.

Yusef bent to help the girl to her feet. She looked up at him with frightened brown eyes. The girl was beautiful. Perhaps eighteen, her silky black hair ran down dark shoulders to a trim waist. A necklace of gold hung across her indigo sarong.

"Are you alright?" Tragon asked.

The girl looked at him in confusion. She spoke some words to Yusef that he repeated somewhat haltingly. The language was a dialect of Jadian, Yusef's native tongue.

"She says she is alright," Yusef said. "And she is grateful."

"I understood," Tragon said. "I've learned enough of your language, that I think I can converse with her. Let's see if she understands me."

In pidgin Jadian, he asked her name. Her eyes widened in surprise and she smiled.

"My name is Oonama." She had a soft lilting voice. "I am princess of the Kagoroa people."

"Where is your village?" Tragon asked.

"There is a trail through the jungle." She shook her head doubtfully. "But we cannot go there. There is much trouble. I have run away to escape the Lai-Lai Thal Zhoon and Daigoro."

She looked back at the jungle and trembled.

"She is very frightened, captain," Yusef said.

Tragon looked at his first mate and saw how intently he gazed at the jungle princess. He'd known Yusef Ali Ahmed Nazir, desert warrior turned first mate of the Orion, for some time — since that day three summers ago, when the Jadian had saved his life in a Xalerian alley, and vowed to serve henceforth as his guardian and protector. He knew him to be a man of solitary habits, not given to wenching or any of the other passions common to men of the sea. He'd never before seen Yusef look at a woman the way he looked at this one.

2

"Daigoro has gone mad," Oonama said. "He killed my father and the man I was to marry. He intended to sacrifice me to the Lai-Lai Thal Zhoon tonight, during the dark of the moon. I cannot return home. There is nothing left for me there now. Nothing but death."

It was late afternoon. The girl sat across the table from Tragon and Yusef in Tragon's cabin. Wine and food sat untouched before her as she told her story.

"Slow down," Tragon said. "Start at the beginning. Who is Daigoro? What is this Lai-Lai Thal Zhoon, or whatever you call it?"

"Daigoro is the Lol-Noi of our village," she said, tossing her silky black hair back from her shoulders. "The high priest of Gorkala, the Thunder God. He is a man of great power. He has the power to call Gorkala's servant, the Lai-Lai Thal Zhoon, down from the mountain – t he devil bird that comes during the Black Moon to feast on the Chosen One. Daigoro says the sacrifice appeases

Gorkala's anger and is all that prevents him from destroying our village. Daigoro says if not for his intervention, and his magic, the people of Kagoroa would long since have ceased to exist."

"You said this Daigoro killed your father?" Yusef asked.

"My father was a good man. A wise man. King of our village. Daigoro hated him because he did not believe what Daigoro said. My father did not believe in Daigoro's magic. One day my father said the people of Kagoroa should kill the devil bird. He said we should stop living in fear of the Lai-Lai Thal Zhoon and Daigoro. Daigoro screamed and cursed at my father. He put a spell on him and said that in two days he would be dead. And in two days he was dead."

Her large, almond-shaped eyes filled with tears and her grief made her unable to speak. Yusef handed her a linen napkin and she dabbed at her eyes.

"How did he die?" Tragon asked.

"One night after supper, he suddenly clutched at his stomach and fell over in pain. He fell into a fever and by dawn he was dead. It was a terrible death of agony."

"Sounds as if he were poisoned," Yusef said.

"I believe he was," Oonama said. "Daigoro claimed it was the power of his curse that killed him. But that evil monster carries many strange potions and elixirs in his bag. I believe he put something into my father's food."

"You said the high priest also killed the man you were to marry?" Yusef prompted.

"Yes. After my father died, Daigoro came to my home many times. Always on some pretext or other. But I could see the way he looked at me. I could feel the way he wanted me. When Wazimi came around, Daigoro would get angry. Wazimi was a sweet boy. Gentle, kind and strong. One night Daigoro came to see me with presents. He said I should be his woman. Wazimi came in. There was a terrible fight. Daigoro cursed him as he did my father. The next day, Wazimi was found in the jungle. They said a leopard had killed him. His body was torn in shreds. But I know it was not a leopard that killed Wazimi. It was Daigoro."

Her eyes narrowed. "When they brought Wazimi's body in from the jungle, I told the people what I suspected. I told them Daigoro was not a man of magic. He did not speak for Gorkala. That my father was right and we should no longer live in fear. Then Daigoro went mad. He ordered me taken to the Sacred Pyramid and held for sacrifice to Gorkala. I was to be the Chosen One for this Black Moon."

"A jealous man's revenge," Yusef muttered.

"I escaped this morning. I didn't know where I would go. I had to get away."

Tragon grunted. "That's not the first time I've heard of a man claiming divine powers to achieve his ends."

"I say we pay this Daigoro a visit," Yusef said. "Maybe we can teach him a lesson."

"No!" Oonama said. "He has turned my people against me. You would not face just him. The people are too afraid to defy him now. Better to never return."

She looked at Yusef imploringly. "He is evil and he knows how to destroy," she said. She put her hand on Yusef's forearm. "You have saved my life, and I am grateful. I would not see any harm come to you. Better to turn your ship and leave here. If you want to help me, take me with you."

Tragon saw the intensity of the gaze Oonama and his first mate shared.

"Oonama," he said, "this is your home. Would you leave it and your people in the grip of a man like Daigoro? Would your father have smiled on such a deed?"

The girl's eyes glistened and faltered. "But what can I do?"

"If you're willing, we can take you back to your village tomorrow and try to help you get back your birthright. Your people need you. If you stand up to Daigoro, they'll see him for what he is."

"You make it sound easy," she said, "because you do not know. I tried to make the people see what he had done to the two men I loved. But they are blind. They would not see."

"It may take a little persuasion," Tragon said. "That's where we come in."

The girl bowed her head. "There is something else."

"What?" Yusef asked.

"I told the people I did not believe in Daigoro's magic. But there is a part of me that is not so sure. I have seen things. Things I do not understand. Perhaps I am wrong. If so, we would be doomed to failure."

"It's all trickery," Tragon said. "I've seen that kind of magic before."

Oonama turned from Tragon and looked deep into Yusef's eyes.

"What do you say?" she asked. "Do you not fear Daigoro's evil magic?"

The Jadian hesitated a moment. "I do not fear it," he said. "But whether Daigoro's magic is real or trickery, we will fight it and defeat it."

The girl seemed to gain some courage from Yusef's words. "Perhaps you are right," she said. "It is wrong of me to abandon my people. If you are willing to help me, perhaps we can succeed. Someone must lead my people out of the dark ways."

3

Tragon sat on the railing by the ship's bow, running a whetstone along the blade of his sword. It was twilight, and streaks of purple and orange colored the sky over the island. Exotic birds called from the darkening jungle. The intense heat of the day had begun to subside, but the humidity was still thick.

Tragon held the blade up for a moment, and the glow of the dying sun glinted off the highly-polished steel. Yusef came on deck.

"She's resting now," he said.

Tragon put the whetstone down and sheathed his sword. Tragon could see a change had come over Yusef.

"She's something, isn't she, captain?" Yusef asked quietly.

"She's very beautiful."

"It's more than that," the first mate said. "There's something else. Even though she comes from a primitive world, she's intelligent. She doesn't believe what everyone else on her island believes. She has courage. Courage to stand up against the darkness."

"That's what's gotten her into trouble."

"I said before that there are things in this world that cannot be named," Yusef said. "There are many dark things. But Oonama has shown me that even though we may fear them, we must stand against them, or the whole world falls into darkness."

"I suppose that's true, Yusef."

"Captain," Yusef said, a sudden urgency in his voice. "Since the day King Caldec put a price on our heads, we've wandered the seas, fleeing our pursuers. But at the same time, we've been looking for something. A new home. Maybe this could be my place."

Tragon smiled. "I can see what the attraction is."

"In all my travels," Yusef said, "never have I met someone like Oonama. From the moment I saw her I felt something happen inside me." The Jadian seemed to struggle to find the right words. "We have sailed together now many moons," he said. "Shared many adventures. According to the beliefs of my people, the day I saved your life in Xaleria, I became responsible for it, and vowed to safeguard it. I have no choice now but to ask you to release me from that promise. I will be sad to see you sail away, my friend, but if Oonama will have me, I will stay with her."

Tragon was stunned.

"I've never seen you this way," he said. "Are you sure you know what you're doing?"

"More sure than I've ever been about anything. One searches the world for his destiny, and I have found mine."

Tragon could see the deep conviction in Yusef's eyes.

"Then you have my blessing, though it will be a hard parting," Tragon said. "And I wish you and your new found love luck. But before that, we will have to deal with this evil witch doctor."

Yusef's face darkened. "We will deal with him," he said. The steel of his blade sang out as he freed his sword from the scabbard. The last light of the orange sun flashed on the steel.

4

That night, after they'd eaten, Tragon posted sentries on deck and on the beach. Oonama warned him that Daigoro would come to make good his threat to sacrifice her. Tragon gave her his cabin to sleep in; he and Yusef set up small tents on deck where they could sleep. The other crew slept either on the beach or in hammocks down in the hold.

Tragon slept soundly for several hours, but in the middle of the night something awakened him. He opened his eyes to find a strange mist all around him. The air was filled with a sickly sweet fragrance. Through the open flap of the tent he could see the moon rising over the volcano. Then a shadow moved next to him.

He looked up and saw a tall, well-built black man standing over him. A leopard's head was perched on top of his own. The cat's skin draped across his shoulders, and he wore the leopard's clawed paws like gloves. The man wore a black loincloth, and carried a long stick with a cobra carved at the top. A leather bag hung from a strap across his chest. He bent down toward Tragon, and the moonlight lit a cunning smile. Tragon knew he was looking into the face of Daigoro.

He saw two dark shadows steal across the deck and go down the hatch toward his cabin. What had happened to his sentries? How did the witch doctor and his men get on board? He tried to call to Yusef, but found he could only move his mouth and tongue very slowly; he was unable to make any sound. Then he saw Daigoro reach into the leather bag. The hand came out and swung in an arc over him. A cloud of sparkling dust billowed, and the sickening fragrance was suddenly stronger, cloying at his throat.

The witch doctor smiled down at him evilly and turned as the two shadows came up from the hatch, with Oonama in their grasp. Tragon saw the girl struggle, and then was aware that Yusef had awakened beside him. The black man sat up and reached out a hand as if in slow motion.

The witch doctor joined the two men who had the girl. He showered her with the sparkling dust and the girl ceased resisting. Tragon struggled to his feet, and tried to run after them. He heard Yusef hollering incoherently. The deck of the *Orion* suddenly seemed ten leagues long. Every step was a mighty effort. Tragon felt he was running uphill in a dream.

Silent as the darkness, the three men went over the side with the girl. When Tragon finally reached the port rail, he looked out over the moonlit beach and the jungle and saw no one.

Oonama and her kidnappers had vanished.

5

"At least the witch doctor's dust didn't slow us for long," Tragon said, splashing water from the rain barrel on his face. Yusef threw fresh water on himself.

Tragon felt his normal strength returning. Out on the beach, his crewmen were diving into the waves that lapped ashore, to wash themselves of the mind-altering powder.

"It smells like the Sleeping Witch plant," Yusef said. He dipped his head in the barrel and lifted it out, water streaming down his face.

From deep in the jungle came the sound of drums. Tragon saw that the eastern edge of the full moon was beginning to disappear. The Black of the Moon had begun and, if he surmised correctly, the people of Kagoroa had started the ritual sacrifice to the Lai-Lai Thal Zhoon, that Oonama has described. Tragon strapped on his sword, while Yusef slung his quiver of arrows over his shoulder and grabbed the longbow hanging from the mast.

"They can't be too far ahead," Tragon said. "Don't worry.

We'll get her back."

He turned to the crew now assembled on the deck. "I want ten men," he said. "The rest of you wait here."

Minutes later they marched single-file through dank jungle, following the abductors' trail. The path twisted through dense foliage. The air was more humid in the jungle's interior. The smell of thick, rotting vegetation filled Tragon's nostrils. Drops of moisture fell from big dark leaves, catching fragments of the failing moonlight that filtered down through the misty trees.

The drumming and the sound of primitive wind instruments grew louder as they approached Oonama's village. They came to a clearing finally and Tragon signaled for a halt. They crouched in the vegetation.

Ahead, Tragon saw a small village, made up of about twenty-five dome-shaped buildings that formed a broad circle along the perimeter of the clearing. The buildings seemed to be made of some form of clay. In the middle of the clearing the people of Kagoroa danced wildly around a stone pyramid that stood about thirty feet high. The top of the pyramid was flat, and a small squat altar rose from its center. Tragon saw Daigoro climbing stone steps toward the pyramid's height. Oonama lay limply in his arms.

Daigoro reached the top of the stairs, walked across the flat surface and placed Oonama on the altar. He fastened leather thongs on the girl's wrists and ankles, then raised his head and hands to the moon. The crowd below ceased their celebration and became silent. Tragon saw that at least one quarter of the silver moon was now black.

Tragon reckoned there were close to two hundred people assembled around the high altar, at least half of them men armed with spears and knives. He'd brought ten men, and there were only fifteen more back on the *Orion*. He could send back for them, but still they would be vastly outnumbered. It was a situation that called more for brains than brawn. The silence of the night was suddenly broken by a voice that seemed to come from the rotted throat of one long dead and buried.

"People of Kagoroa," Daigoro called out. "Hear me speak! Many changes have occurred. Our king was taken from us, young Wazimi was found dead in the jungle, and a strange madness seized Oonama, the king's daughter, causing her to say evil things of your High Priest. It is as if a curse has been put on the Kagoroa people."

Tragon was distracted when he saw Yusef fit an arrow to his bow. He grabbed his first mate's arm.

"Wait," he said.

"Let me kill him," Yusef said anxiously. "I've heard enough." Tragon saw the anguish his first mate was feeling.

"Hold steady."

"People of Kagoroa," Daigoro continued, "what has befallen has been the will of the mountain god Gorkala. Gorkala has watched us, my people, and he has been displeased. He watched Lomara rule as our king, and did not like what he saw. Now he demands that we make amends. Look!"

He pointed up at the eclipsing moon with his cobra stick.

"He takes the queen of the night from us, and it is time we make offering to Gorkala's servant, the Lai-Lai Thal Zhoon. He will come and feast on our offering of Oonama, and remove from our people the last trace of the blood of Lomara and his tribe. I have been your leader in things of the spirit. But it is the will of Gorkala that I, Daigoro, become your leader in all things. He wishes me to be your priest-king. Will you obey the will of Gorkala? What say you, my people?"

The witch doctor's chicanery made Tragon's blood boil. He could see beads of perspiration glinting on the Jadian's body, and sensed the desperation the black man felt. If they were going to rescue the girl, there was only one way. He stepped into the clearing.

"I say that Daigoro is a teller of lies," he shouted, "and is not fit to lead a pack of dogs!"

A clamor rose among the Kagoroa as Tragon approached them. Yusef walked at his side and the rest of the men followed.

"Who dares speak thus to Daigoro!" The witch doctor's eyes burned with fury when he saw them approaching. He pointed his cobra stick at them. "Kill them!"

Tragon saw a man preparing to throw a spear, but an arrow shot out suddenly from Yusef's bow and struck the shaft of the spear, knocking it from the man's hands. The crowd gasped.

"Daigoro is a fake," Tragon shouted. "He needs you, people of Kagoroa, to do his killing for him. He uses the powder of the Sleeping Witch plant to work his so-called magic. All he has told you are lies."

"Kill them, kill these strangers!" Daigoro screamed in rage. "They are the ones who tried to take Oonama away. They are the ones who wanted to deprive the Lai-Lai Thal Zhoon of his prize tonight. They would offend Gorkala and bring down his mighty wrath on us!"

Confusion and fear froze the villagers. Tragon and his men walked through the crowd of stunned people and made their way toward the altar. The men and women stood silently, their eyes suspicious, their weapons ready. Tragon knew one false step would mean their doom.

"I say that Daigoro has no magic," Tragon said. He reached the bottom of the steps and started up, with Yusef behind him. "Only tricks. Tricks he uses to fool the people of Kagoroa. Oonama told us her story. About the curse Daigoro put on her father and the man she loved. But they did not die from magic. Daigoro killed them."

Tragon and Yusef reached the top of the pyramid and looked across the altar at the witch doctor. Oonama lay on the marble altar slab, her eyes half-closed. She moved restlessly.

"Examine the claws on the leopard skin he wears," Tragon said. "They killed Wazimi. And search in Daigoro's bag - there you will find the poison he fed to Lomara."

Now the Kagoroas looked up at the witch doctor, and raised their voices in question.

"Silence!" Daigoro commanded, raising his cane. The crowd hushed. He glared at Tragon with eyes full of hate. "Who are you, strangers?"

"I am Tragon of Ramura and this is Yusef Ali Ahmed Nazir, men who do not believe in your magic, evil one."

Daigoro's eyes ran over them and his lips twisted in a grim smile.

"You say Daigoro has no magic," he said. "That he tells lies. But it is you who lie. For if I have no magic, how is it then that at this moment, in this very place, I can summon Gorkala's servant, Lai-Lai Thal Zhoon? Behold!"

The witch doctor raised his serpent-shaped stick. Tragon looked up and saw that the moon was now in total shadow and the night was suffused with a strange gray light. Then even the shadow of the dark moon was suddenly blotted out. Tragon felt a chill down his spine as he heard the sound of large wings flapping overhead. He felt the wind they made as a huge flying thing suddenly hovered over the altar, blocking the eclipsed moon from his view.

"The Lai-Lai Thal Zhoon!" Daigoro screamed. "Kill them! Kill the unbelievers. Feed their bones to Gorkala so that the people shall know the truth of my magic!"

Tragon had never seen anything like the monstrosity above him. Leathery wings with a span of at least thirty feet beat the air. A long narrow beak snapped loudly. Flaming red eyes glared at him. Tragon pulled his sword from it sheath.

"Free the girl," he told Yusef. The Jadian ran to Oonama, but Daigoro leapt in his way and brandished his serpent staff. Fury propelled Yusef. His shoulder jarred the witch doctor, the charge toppling Daigoro down the steps. Then Yusef slashed the thongs binding Oonama's wrists and ankles. The girl opened her eyes and rose sluggishly.

Tragon swung his sword at the sky creature's legs and taloned feet. The long narrow beak darted and pecked at him. The red eyes glowed as the monster swooped and hovered over the altar, attempting to grab him with beak and claw. Fierce cries that might have come from a giant crow shredded Tragon's ears.

Then Tragon heard Yusef's bow twang and an arrow struck the flying reptile in its neck. The monster shrieked in pain and landed on top of the pyramid. Tragon stepped in and thrust his sword in the thing's chest. The Lai-Lai Thal Zhoon flapped its wings, and pounced on him. Razor-sharp talons dug into Tragon's shoulders and he felt himself being lifted into the air. He stabbed upward, but could not reach the creature's breast. He hacked at its leg again, and saw two more arrows strike the creature in the chest. It screamed in rage. Tragon saw the ground receding still further below him as the monster tried to fly away. But Yusef's arrows were having their effect. The flying horror suddenly faltered and then plummeted to the ground.

Tragon rolled free, avoiding the sharp beak that snapped at him. He ran in with his sword and plunged it deep into the creature's heart. With a final shriek the monster's head dropped on the ground and it lay still. The Lai-Lai Thal Zhoon was dead.

Tragon's crew gathered around him at the base of his pyramid. He caught his breath while the Kagoroas stood in fear and awe.

"You see," Tragon said. "No magic. Only a flying creature that could be killed. Daigoro has used fear and superstition to rule you, to make you obey his will. There is nothing to fear."

"Do not listen, my people," Daigoro said, regaining the top of the pyramid. "This blasphemer brings only destruction for himself and those who heed his words. Obey the will of Gorkala and kill these strangers - or the god of the fire mountain will destroy us all!"

"More empty words," Tragon said.

"My words have power," Daigoro said. "Witness the power of Daigoro!"

The witch doctor threw his stick at Tragon. As it flew, the carved serpent head came alive. Venom-dripping fangs sought Tragon's throat. The sight made Tragon's hair stand on end, but he moved instinctively. When the cobra's fangs were nearly on him, he swung his sword and decapitated the hissing serpent. The snapping jaws lay at his feet in the dirt. Its body writhed blindly nearby.

Daigoro pulled the knife that hung at his side and lunged at Oonama. Yusef sprang in front of her, grabbed the witch doctor's wrist, and twisted it.

"Enough of you, witch doctor," Yusef said, twisting the wrist until Daigoro was forced down on his knees. Yusef forced the blade toward the priest's chest. The witch doctor glared up at him.

"Kill me, and all Kagoroa dies with me," he said through gritted teeth. "Gorkala will awaken the Mountain of Fire."

There was a last moment of hesitation. Yusef felt the temptation to weaken and succumb to the witch doctor's threat. Did he have such power? Then he saw steel flash as Daigoro's other hand came up with a smaller dagger. Before the blade could strike, Yusef thrust the knife into the man's chest. The witch doctor collapsed.

Tragon looked at the people of Kagoroa, who stared in confusion. He knew it was a turning point for the people of this island, who had lived so long in fear and darkness.

Atop the pyramid, Yusef strode forward with Oonama by his side. Above them the light of the moon returned, its pale silvery beams shining down. The Black of the Moon was ending. Oonama raised her hands to the crowd.

"People of Kagoroa," she said. "The words of the strangers are true. Daigoro was an evil man. He killed my father and Wazimi, and everything he did was for his own selfish reasons. We no longer have to live by his lies. We are free to live as we wish now. Thanks to these men."

"Brothers and sisters of Kagoroa," Yusef said. "Here before you is Oonama, the true and rightful ruler of this beautiful island. Take her back in your hearts and let her wisdom guide you to a brighter future."

There was a silence for one tense moment. Then someone shouted. "Hail Oonama! Hail Queen!"

Oonama looked up at Yusef in the waxing moonlight as the people of Kagoroa shouted and danced again.

"We have known each other not even a day," she said. "But I feel I have known you a lifetime."

Yusef looked down at the beautiful cinnamon girl. But before he could speak a deafening explosion and bright light lit the night. A huge ball of fire shot into the sky from the volcano, and a dark cloud of ash billowed out. At the volcano's height they saw the red glow of lava.

"Gorkala!" a man in the crowd screamed. "It is as Daigoro said - Gorkala has awakened the Mountain of Fire!"

There was another explosion. A red fireball tore through the air and into the jungle nearby. A red glow grew in the darkness of the forest.

"Now we will all die!" the man in the crowd shouted. The ground shook. A third fireball thundered from the mountain and smashed into the side of the pyramid. Sparks and flames showered over the crowd. Small fires began to eat the nearby huts.

"No," Oonama shouted. "This is not Daigoro's doing."

"It is her fault," another in the crowd shouted as the ground shook beneath their feet. "Oonama brought this on us! She dared challenge the will of Daigoro. Now we will all pay!"

The crowd screamed as the earth moved.

"She must die," someone shouted. "Kill her!"

"My people!" Oonama shouted. "Please listen -"

From the midst of the crowd a spear flew upward. Oonama's body jerked. She cried out in pain and collapsed, her slender fingers clutching at the shaft that protruded between her breasts.

"Oonama!" Yusef shouted. He knelt and clasped her tightly in his arms.

She looked up at him as if from a far distance. "For a moment there was hope," she whispered, "but it was not to be. It was as I feared. Daigoro's magic was too strong."

"No!" Yusef cried.

"Hold me-"

Her head fell back.

Yusef stared at her, then rose to glare down at the mob, searching for the man who had thrown the spear. Suddenly another explosion launched a fourth ball of fire. It arced across the black sky and smashed into the crowd, creating a human inferno of twisted, screaming bodies. Some of the villagers died instantly, some burned and the rest ran in screaming panic. Flame and cinders filled the air.

Yusef stood, seemingly unable to move. Tragon looked down and saw the people of Kagoroa running as the ground shook and red sparks flew like fireflies all around them. Their homes were burning and they had become like frightened, savage animals. Babies and small children were trampled as adults ran for their lives, screaming prayers to Gorkala. He looked over at his grief-stricken first mate and at the dead princess at his feet.

"I'm sorry, my brother," he said "There's nothing we can do for her now. Hurry. It's too late to save this place. We must get to the ship and save ourselves."

Yusef looked at him. The volcano's crimson light reflected in his glistening eyes. "He told me that if I killed him all Kagoroa would die with him. Did he call this down? Were we wrong?"

Tragon saw the bright red lava pour over the rim of the volcano. It would soon overrun the jungle and bury the village. The whole island of Kagoroa might well crumble and fall into the dark sea. For a moment he wondered. Had Daigoro brought this on?

"It's a coincidence, Yusef," he shouted over the rising din of terror below. He tried to shut off the icy sensation of fear that had begun to gnaw at his reason. "That's all. Just a coincidence. What else could it be?"

THE DACUNA

Thirty days becalmed. Thirty blistering days the *Orion* sat in the fetid waters of the Sargasso Sea. Never had Tragon of Ramura, captain of the *Orion*, seen the like. He looked out over the deck of the ship at his men lying parched and burned, their hands still gripping the oars they could no longer row. They had run out of fresh drinking water two days ago and now they lay sick and dying.

”It's no use, Captain.” Yusef Ahmed Ali Nazir, the first mate, wiped sweat from his shaved head. “Unless there is a miracle, we are done for.”

Tragon looked at the black man from Jadia, and saw despair on his first mate's countenance.

“We never should have entered these waters,” Yusef said. “The old soothsayer in Kabula was right. He warned us not to try to reach Zaguro by this route. We laughed at his dire words. He said the day would come when we would look in the sky and see the Dacuna circling over us high in the sky–the giant bird that eats the flesh of dying sailors.”

Tragon turned his eyes skyward.

“There's nothing in the sky yet, Yusef,” he said.

There was a loud trumpeting and the splashing of water. Everyone turned sternward. Tragon's grey eyes narrowed at the sight that met his gaze. A beast of a sort that he had never seen before was moving toward them in the water. It was nearly half the size of the *Orion*. Its body was shaped like that of a whale, but a long dorsal fin trailed down its back, and two gigantic tusks jutted down from its upper jaw. The creature dove, thrashing the water, with a wide tail covered with long, vicious looking spikes.

"On your feet, men," Tragon ordered.

Galvanized by fear, the crew struggled up from their oars and gathered their weapons. Spears and swords were soon in hand as they waited for the beast to resurface. The creature rose up through the boiling water and struck the ship's prow with its head. The *Orion* shuddered.

Tragon ran to the port side with a spear and threw it at the glistening beast's hide. Yusef stood next to him with his long bow and let three arrows fly in quick succession. If the monster even noticed, it gave no outward sign. The thing turned and began circling back.

"Brace yourself," Tragon shouted. He grabbed another spear from one of the crew and stood on the bulwark. Two more arrows struck the beast's head. The huge jaws opened and it moved forward, its giant tusks ready.

Tragon hauled back and heaved the spear. It flew into the dark maw of the creature's mouth. The massive jaws slammed shut, breaking the spear in two. The sea-beast's forehead rammed the *Orion* and the ship rebounded with the sound of crunching wood. The beast dove down again into the depths.

"One more like that and we'll be sunk," Tragon said.

The Jadian first mate stood searching the water to see where the sea-beast would resurface. Then, suddenly, Takira, one of the crew, cried out.

"The Dacuna!" he screamed. He pointed skyward. "Aaiiieee! The Dacuna! All is lost!"

Tragon looked up and saw the dreaded carrion bird circling high over the ship. Its huge wings, wider than twice the length of the *Orion*, stretched out over the windless sky and the bird glided silently in the dead air in a tight circle over the ship.

"It knows we are doomed," Takira said. "It waits for the sea-beast to kill us and then the Dacuna will come for our remains."

"It hasn't killed us yet," Tragon hollered.

But then, he saw the monster-fish again steaming straight for them. Tragon could see its tiny eyes glaring at him with malevolent hatred. Tragon mounted the bulwark again, another spear in hand. But this time the monster turned suddenly, raised its spike-covered tail in the air, and slammed it hard against the ship. Wood splintered. The impact of the attack sent Tragon flying backward onto the deck.

"We'll never stand another onslaught," he hollered at Yusef, as he got to his feet. But Yusef seemed not to hear him. The Jadian was busy tying a long line of rope to the end of one of his arrows.

"What are you doing?"

Making sure the line was secure, Yusef fitted the arrow to the bow.

"I have an idea," he said. "Try to hold the sea-beast off."

The black man raised the bow high. Tense muscles rippled under his black skin. The arrow shot straight up, towing the rope behind it. The Dacuna seemed oblivious to the missile speeding its way. When the arrow struck, Yusef dropped the bow and grabbed the line attached to the arrow.

"That should hold," he said, tying the rope around the mainmast

Everyone onboard watched as the Dacuna's mighty wings began to flap. It let out a terrible cry of pain. The mast creaked under the strain of the rope, but slowly the *Orion* began to move in the water.

A trumpeting blast came from the port side, as the sea-beast charged the ship again. This time every man on board, strengthened by Yusef's miraculous feat, ran to the side. Spears, knives, swords, pikes–everything the could find–they threw at the monster. Blood came pouring from its mouth, and it backed away.

"We're away," Takira shouted. "Yusef has saved us!"

Tragon looked up at the Dacuna, wings now steadily flapping, pulling the ship toward the west.

"An amazing shot, Yusef," Tragon said.

"According to the legend," Yusef said, "when the Dacuna knows it will die, it must fly to Carmush, the island home of its birth. It was our only chance to get away from the sea beast, and I prayed that my aim would be true enough. We should reach fair winds before long."

THE KING OF SORANGO

1

The pale light of a gibbous moon shone down on empty streets and dark, silent houses. Tragon of Ramura, Captain of the *Orion*, stood in the center of the main street of Sorango— a city that was not at all the way he remembered it. The intersection ahead should have had people in it, but there was no one. There was an eerie stillness in the night air and a silence that was both oppressive and foreboding.

"What do you make of it, captain?"

Tragon looked over at the solidly built black man, who stood next to him, bow and arrow at the ready. Yusef Ali Ahmed Nazir, the desert warrior from Jadia, had served these past two years as Tragon's first mate. Behind him stood ten swarthy men armed with sword, dagger, and bludgeon – men selected from the crew of the *Orion.*

"No one on the streets, no one on the docks when we sailed in," Tragon said. "Where is everyone?"

Suddenly a woman's scream shattered the silence from just beyond the moonlit intersection ahead.

"This way," Tragon said, running ahead. The crew followed close on his heels.

They ran to the intersection and paused momentarily,

shocked by the scene taking place half way up the street. A young woman clad in a tightly-girdled tunic stood with four men battling for their lives amidst a snarling, slavering pack of giant anthropoid-like creatures. One man lay on the ground, either dead or unconscious. There were four of the monsters, each much larger than the humans they were attacking. Their fierce growls and grunts filled the air, as the men tried to fend off their savage attack with swords.

One of the apes grabbed a man standing in front of the girl. The beast picked him up, grabbed his head with one giant claw-like hand, gave it a vicious twist, then tossed the lifeless body to the ground. The creature lumbered forward, brushing aside the men that tried to intervene. The woman screamed and struggled as the monster grabbed her with a hairy arm and hoisted her over his shoulder.

In the moonlight, Tragon recognized her. She had grown up since he'd last seen her, but there was no mistaking the golden hair and beautiful face. She was Davinia, daughter of Lychos, the noble ruler of the city. Without hesitation, he charged forward. The creature turned at the sound of his footsteps, and a mighty arm swung out. The impact was shattering. Tragon flew back, crashing into the wall of a building. The ape pounded its massive chest with its free hand, a deafening roar rumbling up from its throat.

Tragon picked himself up as the eight-foot tall beast lumbered toward him in a low crouch. Keeping his weight on the balls of his feet, Tragon lunged at the creature and plunged the tip of his sword into its side. The beast roared and made a grab for him. Tragon withdrew the bloody blade and dodged the massive hand. The creature put a hand over the wound, and stood for a moment as if surprised by the pain it felt. Tragon jumped in closer, sending his blade deep into the monster's belly. The ape screamed again, dropping the girl roughly on the ground. It pounded on the pavement with its massive fists, then lumbered forward with a roar.

Tragon swung his blade, but the animal's onslaught was

too forceful, too deliberate. Mighty arms like steel cables locked around Tragon's torso. The monster lifted him off the ground and he felt his ribs being crushed. His arms were free, but the pain of the monster's vise-like grip was paralyzing. The hideous odor of the ape's breath steamed in Tragon's face as the monster's arms tightened around him. The moon overhead began to swim before Tragon's eyes, as he felt the life being crushed out of him.

Then suddenly the beast yelled in pain and Tragon felt the grip of the mighty arms loosen. He was vaguely aware of Davinia standing behind the ape, a sword belonging to one of the dead men in her hands, thrust now into the monster's side. Able to breathe again, Tragon grasped the hilt of his own sword with both hands and lifted it over the ape's head. With a savage grunt, he drove the blade point-first straight down into the top of the ape's skull. Blood spurted and a horrendous scream rose up into the humid night sky. The hairy arms let go of Tragon and the beast fell. Tragon pulled the blade free and jumped clear, as the ape collapsed dead in the street.

He ran to the girl, who stared at him in disbelief.

"Is it really you?" she asked. "It's a miracle."

Tragon turned and saw Yusef and his men battling for their lives with the three remaining apes. Yusef stood with bow drawn as one of the anthropoids charged. An arrow flew and struck the animal in the chest. The creature staggered back, looked down curiously at the wooden shaft protruding from his hairy thorax. It let out a roar and was about to resume its charge when a horn sounded. Its eerie call came from the mountains on the other side of the jungle that lay at the edge of the city. It called again— a strange primitive cry. To his amazement, Tragon saw the three remaining apes turn and lope off down the street. He watched as they disappeared into the darkness at the edge of the jungle.

"Tragon," the girl said. "I don't know what brings you to Sorango at this very moment, but thank the gods you're here."

"What has happened?" Tragon asked. "What were those creatures?"

"We can't talk here," she said. "To linger on the streets of

Sorango after dark is to seek death."

Yusef came over to them, followed by a young, dark-haired man in a red tunic.

"Davinia," the man said. "Are you all right?"

"Yes, Dagar," she said. "I'm fine." Tragon noted the gentle tone in her voice and the look in her eye when she spoke to the young man.

"I'd like you to meet someone, Tragon," she said. "This is Dagar. He is Chief Procurator of Sorango, a nobleman, and my fiancé."

"I thank you, stranger," the man said, clasping his arm. "For saving my betrothed, I owe you more than I can ever pay."

Tragon looked in surprise at the girl.

"So the young girl I knew has grown into a woman and is about to marry," Tragon said. "Your father must be a happy man."

The girl suddenly became crestfallen.

"He was happy when he heard the news," she said. "But whether he is happy now, or even whether he is dead or alive, I do not know. Terrible things have befallen Sorango, Tragon."

He waited for her to tell more but instead she looked around at the dark shadows. Her companions picked their two fallen comrades up from the street.

"Come to my father's palace," she said, "and I will explain."

Tragon nodded and followed her lead. Yusef signaled to the crew and they started up the street at a brisk pace.

2

"It is all too horrible to believe," Davinia said. "The monsters you saw tonight are the servants of an evil being who has kidnapped my father."

They were in a private chamber of the palace. Tragon sat across a large oak table from Davinia and Dagar. Yusef sat at Tragon's side. Food and wine had been brought. The men from the ship's crew had been taken to the main dining hall for refreshment.

"They tried to abduct me as we were returning to the palace from a prayer vigil for my father at the Temple of Amara," the girl continued.

"Where is your father being held?" Tragon asked.

"They took him somewhere up in the mountains," she said, brushing a blonde curl back from her forehead. "Where exactly we know not. We sent an expedition up there to find him three days ago and they have not returned. Tomorrow I will lead another force to the mountains myself."

"Please, Davinia," Dagar interrupted. "I've told you that I will lead that party tomorrow and you will remain in the palace, where it is safe."

"And I've told you, Dagar, that if you want a wife who sits like a wilting lily when there's trouble about, you perhaps had better find another woman. My father, if he is still alive, is in grave danger, and I will go to his rescue. I can handle sword and axe as well as any man, as you well know."

Dagar looked chagrined. He turned to Tragon.

"Can you reason with her?" he said.

"She's always had her own mind," Tragon said. "But stop arguing for now and tell me what this is all about."

"It all began about two weeks ago," Dagar said. "Men began disappearing from the city. Lychos set up sentries, but still the kidnappings continued. Fear ran wild. Shopkeepers closed early, mothers took their children in at sundown. No one ventured out on the streets after dark."

Davinia handed Tragon a yellowed parchment. "Three nights ago, mysteriously, this note appeared on the palace door," she said.

Tragon glanced at the strange writing.

"It's written in the ancient language of Sorango," Davinia said, "but the temple priests were able to read it. It says 'On the night of the next full moon, Xenophan the Great returns to reclaim his domain. He requires more slaves to work in the Temple of Iscahar to prepare for the birth of the New Kingdom. Send them into the forest at dawn or suffer the consequences.'"

"Xenophan?" Yusef asked.

"That is a name that was given to only one man in all of history, Yusef," Tragon said. "And that man died a thousand years ago, if indeed he ever lived. I've always thought he was just a myth."

"At first we thought it was some kind of hoax," Dagar said. "How could such a thing be possible? Xenophan was a mad warrior-king who ruled the world with an army of giants, living only to satisfy his passion for gold. He raided and plundered kingdoms, amassing a huge treasure. He conquered our ancient ancestors here in Sorango. But it proved to be his last conquest. He fell victim to his own greed and lust. He was seduced by Queen Taria, who was said to be the most beautiful woman in the world. Xenophan fell for her charms and she rendered him unconscious with a potion. While he slept, Taria had the high priest read an ancient curse that, with the aid of the potion, placed him in a state of perpetual slumber.

"She took him to the ancient temple of the goddess Iscahar high in the mountains. She had chests of Xenophan's gold melted into molten liquid, put Xenophan in a marble sarcophagus and had the gold poured over him. For ten centuries he remained asleep in his golden tomb."

"The location of his tomb and Iscahar's temple was long lost to antiquity," Davinia explained. "Xenophan had been all but forgotten by our people. Not knowing if Xenophan had really returned, or if the note and the kidnappings were some sort of plot, father called a meeting of the Council of Nobles. The next morning on his way to the meeting, he was attacked on the road. One survivor from his retinue returned to tell us what happened. He told of the apes seizing my father and of something even more incredible. He said the apes were led by something not human. They obeyed the commands of a man made entirely of gold! The ancient evil has returned. Xenophan is risen from the dead literally transformed into the thing he lusted after most in life. He has become a living mummy of gold."

The girl shuddered suddenly. Dagar put his arm around

her.

"Tomorrow night the moon is full," Davinia said. "If Xenophan spoke the truth, his evil reign will rise again from the ashes. In the morning we will go to the mountain. We must find the hidden temple before it's too late, rescue Lychos and stop Xenophan from carrying out his plan."

"And I will go with you," Tragon said. "Lychos was a good friend to me, when I needed one. Time to repay the debt." He looked over at Yusef, who had been listening intently.

"What do you say, Yusef?"

"I think I would like to find this temple," the ebony warrior said quietly. The gold circle that dangled from his ear flashed in the light of the torches that lit the room. "And I would like to see this Xenophan. I have seen mummies before. But not one that was alive. And especially not one made of gold."

3

Tragon jumped up with a start from the bed. Something had awakened him from a sound sleep. He looked around in the dark at unfamiliar surroundings. He was in an apartment in the palace. He heard a woman's scream and a wild commotion coming from Davinia's quarters. He saw Yusef rising from a bed on the other side of the room. Tragon grabbed the sword he'd left on the floor next to the bed and bolted from the room, Yusef right behind him. In the hallway, he saw two soldiers lying unconscious outside Davinia's door. He ran into the room. Furniture was overturned and another man lay bleeding on the floor. He was pointing toward the open window.

"The monsters," he said. "They took her. I tried to stop them, but they were too strong."

The guard collapsed to the floor. Tragon ran to the window and stepped out on the balcony. The moon was low in the sky now but there was still enough moonlight to see the streets below. Dark shadows turned a corner several blocks away.

Dagar ran into the room, his face pale.

"What's happened?"

"We've no time to waste," Tragon said. "Xenophan's pets have taken Davinia. There should have been more guards here."

"I'll assemble my soldiers."

"No time for that," Tragon said. "I'm going after them now."

Just then the captain of the palace guard ran into the room.

"Captain, assemble your men," Dagar shouted at him. "Follow our trail as soon as you can."

Tragon turned to Yusef.

"Get our men and the rest of the crew and join the captain and his men, Yusef," he said.

"No, captain," Yusef objected, a deep frown on his ebony brow. "I go with you."

"Better if you and the King's guard all come together in force. We don't know what we may face."

"May Khemur be with you," the Jadian said, touching his finger tips to his chest and forehead.

"Let's go," Tragon shouted to Dagar. He ran out onto the balcony and leapt over the balustrade, landing on soft grass some ten feet below. Dagar followed. Tragon ran toward the corner where he'd seen the shadows disappear. When they got there he realized he was back on the main street they had traversed earlier. He looked ahead and saw only empty street running up to the edge of the jungle at the far end of the city.

"They are already in the forest," Dagar said.

They dog-trotted up the street until the brick paving ran out and their feet pounded on dirt. The road became a narrow trail through high razor grass and soon the buildings of Sorango faded into the darkness behind them and ahead were the dark, menacing shadows of trees and hanging vines. They followed a narrow path of broken twigs and crushed leaves left by the apes. But after a few hundred yards all spoor suddenly disappeared. Tragon stood there looking around for some telltale clue.

"They must have taken to the trees," he said. "Where does this trail lead?"

"To Mount Ska. Come on. We should be able to pick their trail up once they take the mountain path."

4

They trekked for several hours through the forest. At times the path seemed to disappear into dense overgrown foliage. But Dagar hacked through the vegetation with his sword and easily found the trail again. As they marched, neither man was aware of the bright yellow eyes that glared at them from behind the dense foliage.

"You know the path well," Tragon said, as they walked in the darkness.

"I've been through here many times as man and boy," the youth said.

"Have you scaled the peaks of Mount Ska as well?"

"Yes."

"Good," Tragon said. "We'll need your knowledge of the mountain passes. If we can't pick up the apes' trail, we may have to search until we find Iscahar's temple."

"We'll find it," Dagar said. "I promise you." Tragon was surprised at the strong conviction in the man's voice.

Without warning a black fury suddenly leapt out of the jungle, and hit Tragon full force. The impact of the heavy body knocked him to the ground. The bright yellow eyes of a Sorangan panther glared down at him, and sharp white fangs sought for his throat. Tragon clutched at the fur around the carnivore's neck with both hands, in an attempt to keep those snapping jaws away. The panther snarled and hissed and Tragon knew next he would feel sharp claws digging into his belly. He saw Dagar a few feet away, standing back, his sword held down at his side.

With a desperate lunge, Tragon forced the animal over on its side, rolled and climbed onto its back. He locked his legs around the panther's belly and encircled its neck with both arms. Exerting all his strength, he squeezed the carnivore's windpipe. The cat screeched and its claws shredded the grass and vegetation under it as it flailed about in rage. Tragon wanted to reach for his sword but fear of releasing his grip on the cat's neck prevented him from trying. The cat's body twisted and heaved in convulsions of fury. The beast tried to leap in the air but only succeeded in rolling onto its back, with Tragon under him.

The panther's underbelly now exposed, and Tragon looked up to see Dagar finally stepping forward, his sword ready. Why didn't he strike? Tragon knew he couldn't hold the animal much longer. Then finally Dagar lunged and thrust the point of his blade into the cat's torso. The panther shrieked in agony, its claws and teeth searching for one last bit of flesh to rend, but finding none. Then it suddenly ceased all motion. Tragon pushed the beast's limp carcass away and got to his feet. All of the jungle seemed deadly still and silent.

Dagar cleaned the panther's blood off his sword with a broad palm leaf. "Sorry, I seemed to hesitate," he said. "I was afraid to strike in case I hit you by mistake."

Tragon had several cuts and scratches but was otherwise all right. He brushed some bloody dirt off his arms and looked at his companion with a frown.

"Better late than never," he said. "We'd better be on our way."

They continued along the tangled trail, but now Tragon was suddenly mistrustful of Davinia's fiancé. From the moment he met Dagar, he'd sensed there was something about the man —something he was trying to hide. Now he was even more suspicious of him. He said nothing, however, and followed Dagar along the path.

5

The grey light of dawn found them standing at the base of the mountain. Tragon was hungry and thirsty. He had hoped to overtake the apes in the jungle and regretted having started out so hastily. He'd brought neither food nor drink. Next to him stood Dagar, and the two men looked up the face of the mountain that rose up some 10,000 feet. The peaks were snowy white at the top —a serene sight, Tragon thought, but one that totally belied the evil that lay inside those craggy peaks.

"Come this way," Dagar said. "There is water."

Tragon followed the man along a narrow trail that angled its way upward perhaps a quarter of a mile along the face of the mountain until it came to a fissure in the granite wall. Dagar stepped into the crevice. Tragon took his sword from its scabbard and swung it. A piece of the mountain rock flew away, leaving a chink in the wall, that he was sure Yusef would see. He followed Dagar into the fissure.

The space was barely wide enough for them to walk. Tragon looked up and could see a sliver of daylight far over his head. They progressed nearly a hundred yards and suddenly the fissure widened out and they found themselves in a canyon. To the right a narrow ribbon of water trickled down the rocks from the snow of the upper peaks and collected in a pool. They walked over to it. Tragon got down on all fours and slaked his thirst. The water was cold and refreshing.

"Glad you know these mountains so well," Tragon said, sitting up now by the side of the pool.

Dagar sat up and wiped his mouth with the back of his hand. "The mountain is honeycombed with canyons, caves and caverns. I explored many of them as a boy," he said.

"And yet in all your explorations you never came across Iscahar's temple?" Tragon asked.

Dagar shook his head. "Time has erased all traces of the temple."

The same sense of uneasiness Tragon had felt back in the jungle, after the fight with the panther, swept over Tragon again.

Dagar looked down into the pool of clear water. "Davinia said you've known her since she was a little girl," he said.

"I first came here on a return voyage to Ramura from a place called Lashmir in the Southern Sargasso Sea," Tragon said.

"I'd been shipwrecked there. The ship that picked me up stopped here and through odd circumstances I met Lychos and his queen Sirana. Davinia was thirteen summers at the time."

"She told me you saved her father from an assassin."

"The second night after I'd arrived, Lychos was on his way alone to the palace. He likes to go about without fanfare or guards. I had come out of a tavern, having consumed a bit too much wine. I saw a man lurking in an alley. I didn't even know who Lychos was when he passed by. But I saw the man step out behind him with a knife in his hand. I jumped him. It was all over in a few seconds."

"You're a brave man," Dagar said, a vague sadness in his soft brown eyes. "A man must be brave in this treacherous world."

Tragon glanced up at him. Something in the tone of Dagar's voice set his nerves on edge. There seemed to be some inner conflict within the man. Tragon continued with his story. "Lychos took me to his palace. He gave me one of his best ships and a crew and sent me back to Ramura with enough gold to buy two more ships, if I wanted them." Tragon stared intently at the young man. "So you see, Dagar," he said very deliberately, "I'm very fond of Lychos and his daughter. I would not like to see them come to any harm."

Dagar looked away in sudden alarm.

"Let's go back," he said, jumping up suddenly. "We'll wait for the others on the trail."

"What is it, Dagar?" Tragon asked. "What's troubling you? You seem to know something about all this that you haven't told. What is it?"

Dagar's eyes suddenly filled with fright.

"No! I know nothing!"

"Speak, Dagar," Tragon said, drawing his sword. "Speak or I swear---"

"It's all gone wrong," Dagar blurted in panic." I didn't mean for this to happen. I— look out!"

There was a sudden shrieking above their heads, and from ledges in the canyon walls overhead, a half dozen giant, furry shapes descended upon them. Tragon drew his sword and found himself swarmed by a fury of hairy arms and legs, sharp claws and teeth. He fought off the anthropoids' attempts to seize his throat, tear at his eyes, and claw at his innards. Fierce growls and screeches deafened his ears, as he swung his blade. The sharp point of his sword found its way into the chest of one of the apes. But then a hairy arm encircled his neck and tightened around his throat. He struggled futilely to free himself from the monster's grip. Steely fingers tightened around his windpipe. Tragon saw Dagar a few feet away already lying on the ground at another ape's feet. Then all went black.

6

Tragon opened his eyes. Stripes of moonlight were painted across the light blue tunic that covered his chest. He jumped up. The moonlight beamed in through the bars of a cage. He reached out for the bars with both hands. Shackles on his wrists clinked as he grasped the thick iron bars and shook them. He put his face up to the bars and saw a scene that made him wonder if he was really awake or still asleep in the midst of some fevered nightmare. A deep canyon dropped down below him. His lifted his eyes. Craggy mountain peaks towered up into the night sky a full 360 degrees around him. The full moon shown down over the peaks. Its light revealed a once ornate temple carved out of the sandstone on the east wall of the canyon. Long centuries of neglect had rendered the temple little more than a vague shadow of what must have been its former splendor. Worn and broken steps, that were carved out of the stone floor of the canyon an eon ago, led up to the front of the temple, where a crumbling altar stood before stone columns. The columns stood dully in the moonlight, and the detailed carvings of animals and ancient gods etched into their surface were now worn flat by time and barely visible. Next to the altar a deep pit had been dug out of the ground. Something that resembled a huge glass lens stood next to the pit.

On the other side of the altar lay a marble sarcophagus. Next to it, a vat perched on an iron stand that was placed over a burning fire. Inside the vat bubbled something that Tragon thought could only be molten gold. Tragon looked up at the night sky. Over everything, the bright full moon cast a ghostly light.

"It is the moon of the Jackal," a voice said.

Tragon turned and saw that Dear was in the cage with him.

"Xenophan will raise his army of giants from that pit you see below," Dagar said. "He will catch the rays of the moon in that lens and awaken the giants from the mists of time. He will be transformed into human form again and seek revenge for an ancient wrong. Then will begin his second reign."

Tragon grabbed the front of Dagar's tunic and pulled him closer.

"Alright!" he said. "It's time you told me how you know so much."

"It's my fault," Dagar said, his eyes wild with panic. "All of it. I know you suspected as much. During one of my explorations of Mount Ska, I discovered this place. The Temple of Iscahar. It was all covered with rock and dirt then. But I knew the place immediately. I found a room in the rear of the ruins where Xenophan's tomb lay hidden. I rolled the stone away from the door and went inside. I found Xenophan lying there on a marble slab. He was as the legend said— as you see him now—made entirely of gold. Next to him was a stone tablet that contained magic words in a language that was ancient and yet at the same time familiar. The tablet warned me not to speak those words. But I could not help myself. It was almost as if I had no will of my own. Perhaps it was Xenophan himself willing me to do it from the world beyond.

"I read the words aloud and Xenophan's eyes slowly opened and I felt his terrible gaze fall on me. I was paralyzed with fear. He rose from the slab and I stood there trembling, realizing too late what I had done. He came toward me. He could have killed me at that moment. But instead he offered me my life, if I agreed to help him."

"And so you betrayed Lychos and the woman you love?" Tragon wanted to smash the man's head against the iron bars.

"He promised me that no harm would come to them,"

Dagar said breathlessly. "He said I and those I loved would share in the glories to come in his new kingdom, if I helped him. All went well until he captured Lychos and learned that he and Davinia are direct descendants of Queen Taria. He went insane. At last, he could have revenge on the progeny of the woman who had made him suffer a living death for 1,000 years. He sent the apes to take her."

"You knew this and still gave no warning?"

"I didn't know what to do," Dagar said. "I told you. I'm not a brave man. I've always been afraid of things. I've tried to hide it from Davinia. Hoping she'd never see the coward I really am. I know a man like you can't understand. You fear nothing. But I'm afraid, Tragon. Afraid of death. Afraid of whatever terrors lie beyond the grave. If I didn't do what Xenophan wanted, he'd have killed me. I didn't want to die. I kept hoping to find some way to stop him. I asked Davinia to leave with me by ship. But she is so headstrong. Nothing I could do could make her leave. And now it's too late. I've betrayed everything that means anything to me. I've even betrayed Xenophan by leading you here. And for my reward Xenophan has thrown me in here with you. Soon we shall both be dead."

Tragon pushed Dagar away angrily. He took hold of the bars again and gave them another shake.

"We've got to find a way out of here," he said.

"There is no way out," he said. "There is a door behind me, but it is locked tight. We won't get out until Xenophan wants us out."

At that moment, the canyon echoed with the eerie cry of the horn that Tragon had heard when he'd first arrived in Sorango. The sound sent an icy trickle down Tragon's spine. He looked down at the temple and saw a sight that boggled his mind. Standing at the top of the temple steps, just before the altar towered a man. From head to foot— including the short skirt he wore, the embossed cuirass that covered his chest and shoulders, and the crown on his head — he was made entirely of gold. He lifted a gold ram's horn to his lips and again that eerie call went out.

In answer, Tragon saw at least twenty of the gigantic apes appear on ledges that ringed the canyon walls. Now he saw that there were caves cut into the sides of the canyon that must have served as habitats for the grotesque anthropoids. The apes raised a cacophony of shrieks and howls as they jumped and pranced along the ledges.

The horn called once more and from behind the temple walls, Tragon saw two more apes emerge. These held chains in their hands and were tugging at something within the interior of the temple. Then Tragon's blood began to boil as he saw that on the other end of those chains were Davinia and her father King Lychos. They were led to two pillars that stood behind the altar and chained to them.

Now the golden man put the ram's horn down and went over to the right side of altar. He stopped next to the large glass lens and gazed up at the moon. His voice boomed out speaking words in a weird, ancient language—a chant that echoed around the canyon walls.

"He invokes the powers from beyond to raise his ghostly horde from the pit," Dagar whispered.

Xenophan's golden hand grasped the gold frame of the lens and tilted it toward the moon. The lens gathered and concentrated the moon's diffuse light into a solid beam. The tightly focused moon ray shot down into the large pit that gaped darkly next to the altar. A strange blue-white mist began to swirl up from the pit's inner darkness.

Xenophan went over to the altar and retrieved his horn. He put it to his lips as the two apes behind him began to pound huge kettle drums with drumsticks made of bone. They beat a consistent, almost hypnotic rhythm as the golden mummy blew those three eerie notes over and over. Then from the white mist of the pit Tragon saw giant warriors on horseback riding up out of the pit. They were ghostlike figures, not solid human flesh. They wore helmets fashioned in grotesque, frightening designs and rode out of the pit four at a time in a seemingly endless parade from hell.

"They are the ghosts of the ancient warriors," Dagar said. "When the ceremony is completed they will become flesh and blood, and Xenophan's new reign of terror will begin."

Soon the canyon floor was filled with a hundred of the fierce apparitions. The ape drummers continued pounding their steady rhythm on the ancient drums.

Tragon was startled from his fascination with the scene being played out before him, by the sound of the cage door opening. Two apes pulled him out of the cage by the chains that bound him. They brought Dagar out and marched them both down a tunnel that angled at a steep slope to the rear of the temple. They were led through a hallway and out onto the dais on the front of the temple, where Davinia and Lychos were chained up. There were no pillars for Tragon and Dagar to be chained to, so the apes stood next to them, holding them like dogs on a leash. Davinia saw them. Her eyes first lit up with joy at the sight of them, but then quickly filled with despair upon realization of the truth of the situation,

"Tragon, Dagar!" Davinia called. "My love, not you too!"

Lychos looked over at Tragon and nodded at him grimly. "Davinia told me you had come, Tragon," he shouted. "I held out some hope until now. I'm sorry, my friend."

Xenophan now came near. It was a sight Tragon had never thought to behold— a golden mummy standing on the steps of an ancient temple before a horde of ghostly giant warriors on spectral horses. The mummy raised a hand, and the last beat of the drums echoed in the sudden silence.

Xenophan walked to the altar and picked up a golden tube about two feet in length that stood in a holder. He opened one end of the tube and carefully extracted an ancient-looking scroll. He unrolled the scroll and studied it momentarily. Then he began to read from it. His words were in the same strange tongue he had been chanting a moment before. Occasionally, he would stop and look up at the moon hovering overhead, and then he returned his eyes to the scroll and read on. As he read, a cloud suddenly covered the moon and a wind whipped through the canyon. He read on and lightning flashed and thunder rumbled across the dark sky. Xenophan's words came out in a weird sing-song. Then two lightning bolts pitch forked down into the canyon and struck him, as deafening claps of thunder shook the place. A cloud of smoke billowed around Xenophan, who stood silent and unmoving. When the smoke cleared, where once stood a golden mummy, now stood a man of flesh and blood—a young man, strong and vital.

He stood in silence for another moment and then rested the scroll down on the altar. He looked up at the ghost warriors waiting on the canyon floor.

"A thousand years ago," Xenophan said in a deep voice and in a language that Tragon could understand, "an evil woman duped a monarch and sentenced him to ten centuries of perpetual torture. Tonight I will exact revenge on the one who carries the blood, the soul-essence, of the woman who tried to destroy me. And then will begin a new reign of death and conquest such as the world has never seen! Bring her!"

One of the apes unchained Davinia from the pillar. She struggled, but the ape dragged her easily toward the open marble sarcophagus. The ape wrapped the chains around her, binding her arms to her sides. Davinia stood next to the casket, looking up in horror at the caldron of molten gold boiling above her.

"As Taria did a thousand years ago, I now begin the ceremony that will seal your doom." He looked out at the spectral army awaiting his command. "Then, my faithful ones, I shall read the words that will transform you into flesh and blood--- the mightiest fighting force the world has ever seen."

Xenophan picked up the ancient scroll again and began to read. The apes began their drumming again. As the strange sounding words floated out into the night, Tragon saw the girl suddenly seem to go into a trance. Her eyes glazed over and her body swayed like a tree in the wind. She began to walk toward the waiting sarcophagus and the vat of molten gold that bubbled above it.

"No!" Dagar screamed. "No!"

With a desperate tug that surprised the ape holding him,

he tore his chains loose from its grip. He swung the heavy iron links over his head and charged Xenophan. The chain struck Xenophan's hand, knocking the scroll free. The ancient papyrus fell to the floor of the dais. Dagar leaped forward and tried to wrap the chains around the ancient king's neck. But he had no inkling of Xenophan's strength. The ancient warrior picked Dagar up bodily and lifted him high over his dead. Davinia awoke from her trance-like state, saw what was happening, and screamed in horror. With a curse, Xenophan threw Dagar through the air. Dagar crashed against the vat containing the molten gold and fell down into the open casket. Glowing liquid gold poured over the edge of the vat, which had been dislodged, and now rested crookedly on its stand. The molten gold poured all over Dagar. He screamed only once and in an instant his struggles ceased as the hot, liquid gold covered him.

Tragon tried to leap forward, but the ape holding his chains was too alert and held him fast. With a growl the anthropoid drew him in closer. A massive fist was raised over his head and Tragon knew death would follow instantly. But no blow landed. From out of nowhere, Tragon heard— Phhfffftt! Phhhffttt!--- and suddenly there were two arrows sticking out of the beast's head. Another pierced its eye. The creature stood paralyzed for a moment, a look of incomprehension on its face and then it toppled over. Tragon looked out and saw a large body of men coming out of the mouth of a tunnel on the other side of the canyon. In the moonlight he could see Yusef and the captain of the King's Guard at the head of several columns of soldiers, and members of the *Orion*'s crew. Yusef fitted another arrow to his bow and he and the men of the King's Guard charged the apes down on the canyon floor.

Tragon saw all this in a flash. He sprang toward Xenophan. The ancient monarch swung a mighty fist. The blow landed on Tragon's chest, knocking him off his feet. Xenophan strode after the scroll that Dagar had knocked from his hand. He needed to finish the incantation and bring his ghostly army to life. Tragon sprung up and dove. He slid on his stomach and snatched the scroll a split second before Xenophan could grab it. Still sliding on his side, with a flick of the wrist, he threw the scroll into the molten gold bubbling in the sarcophagus.

A terrible scream came up from Xenophan as he watched the scroll sink, turn red, burst into flames and dissolve into the molten gold. The revivified king stood motionless, watching the scroll vanish before his very eyes. Tragon got to his feet, ready to attack, but Xenophan only stood there motionless. He turned slowly and Tragon could see that the ancient warlord's face, which had been transformed from gold into a youthful human face, was now suddenly grey and withered. Deep lines and creases appeared and grew deeper and longer as mere seconds of time elapsed. Xenophan's hands shriveled, the skin turning to parchment and then to crumbling dust. The eyes in the decaying head fell from their sockets and Tragon almost retched as he saw black lips fall away from teeth that dropped one by one to the floor. A few seconds later, all that was left standing was Xenophan's armor, which teetered for a moment then clattered to the floor in a cloud of dust.

Tragon looked out into the canyon floor. A chill ran like a cold finger up and down his spine, as he watched all one hundred of the ghost riders vanish like smoke into the night air. The canyon floor was littered with the corpses of dead apes. The small army that Yusef had brought had taken care of them.

Yusef climbed up the temple steps with his bow in his hand.

"By the grace of Khemur, we were on time," he said.

Tragon clasped the Jadian's arm in thanks. Tragon went over to Davinia, who stood gazing in horror at the smoldering sarcophagus. Yusef went over to Lychos to release him from the chains binding him to the pillar. Tragon stood with his arm around Davinia's shoulders. She stared silently, with tears streaking down her cheeks, at the glowing gold in the open tomb, and the man who lay buried under it.

"Did you see, Tragon?" she said. "How brave he was? He gave his life to save me."

Brave? Tragon thought. Had it not been for the man's

cowardice and deception, none of this would have happened. But he saw her grief and the love she felt for Dagar. What good was truth at a moment like this? And besides, at the end, Dagar had managed to conquer his fear of death and tried to save her.

"He died a hero," Tragon said. "How else would the man who would marry the daughter of the King of Sorango meet death?"

THE RED HEART OF DOLFAR

1

"We're going to be torn apart, captain!"

Tragon of Ramura, Captain of the *Orion*, leaned on the tiller with all his weight. It was all he could do to keep his ship upright in the midst of the gigantic seas that tossed the 100-foot craft. He could barely see the big black man who was shouting into his ear through the heavy rain.

"There's no let up in sight," he yelled back to his first mate. "This is no normal tempest. It came upon us from out of nowhere, out of a clear sky."

Yusef Ali Ahmed Nazir had similar misgivings about the storm. He started to say something, but lightning flashed, and a deafening clap of thunder silenced him.

"Make sure the crew are secured, Yusef," the captain ordered. "I don't want to lose anyone."

Yusef nodded his shaved head and moved to obey the captain's command. A huge wave rose up over the bow of the ship, and billowing seawater crashed down over the deck, as he made his way along the lifeline that had been set up from bow to stern. The black man was from the desert country of Jadia. The world of the sea held no allure for him. In fact, his worst fear was that he would someday fall overboard and drown. But strange circumstance and stranger fate had conspired to make him first mate on a sailing vessel, and close friend and protector of its captain. Such were the customs of Jadia, that when a man saves another man's life, he becomes responsible for it.

But now with foaming spray crashing about, Yusef tread carefully, holding onto the lifeline, checking members of the crew who were tied to bulwark, mast, anchor housing—whatever stationary object might serve to secure them. Someone yelled in the roaring darkness ahead. Yusef saw Kalif, a Tunixian, hanging over the side of the *Orion,* desperately holding onto the top of the bulwark.

Yusef moved toward him. Kalif managed to get his forearms over the edge of the bulwark, but Yusef knew the man could not pull himself over without help. With one hand gripping the lifeline, Yusef leaned out and extended his other arm.

"Take my hand," he shouted.

Kalif remained frozen to the side of the ship. "I cannot!" he screamed.

Yusef moved closer to the sailor, pulling the rope line tauter. "Try!"

The Tunixian held onto the bulwark with one arm and reached out with the other. His fingers trembled as they strained to reach the first mate. Pulling the lifeline even tighter, Yusef lunged forward and grasped the man's hand. Muscles bulged in his ebony arm as he pulled Kalif toward him. Suddenly the man screamed. His fingers tightened their grip. Yusef dug his feet into the slippery deck, and gave one last desperate tug. The Tunixian rose up violently over the bulwark and flopped down on the deck, writhing and screaming in agony. Then Yusef saw the cause of the man's agony, and with an involuntary gasp, he shrank back. The lower half of Kalif's body was gone. Blood gushed from the bloody stump of his torso and washed over the deck. His entrails spilled out near Yusef's feet. The black man stood stunned for a moment, staring at the grisly sight. Then Kalif ceased screaming, and lay still.

"Yusef!" The first mate looked up and saw the tall figure of his captain standing next to him. Tragon pointed out to the sea.

"Look!"

The first mate's eyes widened as they looked out into the maelstrom and saw a shark that was at least thirty feet in length circling amidst the tossing seas. Its dorsal fin cut through the foamy crests of the big waves with a speed and ferocity that was frightening.

"The Lion of the Sea," Yusef said. He raised his arm and pointed. "See! More of them!"

Lightning flashed and, amidst the heaving waves, a school of at least ten of the monsters appeared. Their fins plowed white furls in the water as they began to form a menacing circle completely around the ship.

"What madness is this?" Yusef asked "They're surrounding us."

"This is Venora's work," Tragon said.

"Venora!" Yusef gazed at his captain ruefully. "That evil witch! You should have killed her when you had the chance."

"I may yet," Tragon answered. "Or her me."

2

A loud thump shook the single-masted ship, which still tossed like a toy in the swirling waters. The two men struggled to hold onto the rope, nearly losing their footing. There was another crash, louder than the first, and the *Orion* was pushed slightly to port. Wood splintered.

"The damnable creatures are destroying the ship," Tragon shouted. He looked over the half-drowned crew, scattered and tied down on the deck. "Battle stations, you sea dogs. If you don't want to die, cut yourselves loose and grab your spears."

He ran along the rope line to the wooden box that was nailed down next to the poop deck. He tore the lid open and grabbed as many of the spears that lay inside as he could hold and began passing them out to his men.

"What good are these toothpicks against such monsters?" Tarik the Assurian asked.

"Try and see," Tragon said. "Would you die without a fight?"

The man grabbed the spear and strode back along the lifeline, his head down against the spraying water. Twenty men took twenty spears and then struggled to find a place on the deck from which they could launch their weapons. Tragon moved toward the ship's prow. "Tie yourselves to the lifeline!" he shouted to the crewmen. The ship rose up on the inner wall of a gigantic wave, and Tragon braced himself as the ship raced downward on the other side. Ahead he saw Yusef, already tied to the lifeline near the bow. He had his Jadian longbow in hand and a quiver of arrows on his back. Tragon knew the deadly accuracy of the desert chieftain's aim, but wondered how effective the wooden shafts would be on such massive targets.

One of the monstrous fish turned, broke out of the circle and headed straight for the ship. The black man's elbow came back as he drew the bowstring tight. The longbow, made of strong yet pliant layers of wood and antelope horn, bent back, forming a U. There was a "twang" as Yusef let the arrow go. The shark leaped up in the water, as if to take a bite out of the side of the ship. The arrow entered the shark's open mouth and the creature twisted in the air and fell with a huge splash.

A cheer that was barely audible above the roaring sea went up from the men. The cheer died suddenly as one of the sharks struck against the other side of the ship. Tragon heard wood cracking and straining. He turned and stepped forward as far as his tether on the lifeline would allow and threw his spear into the side of the shark as it swam by. The point of the missile pierced the fish's side and Tragon saw blood streaming in the water. The shark tried to swim away, but white teeth flashed and Tragon heard the sound of snapping jaws as another of the sharks attacked the one he had wounded. The two sea-beasts rolled together in the boiling water in deadly combat.

Suddenly, a weird sound, like the call of some ancient horn, barely audible over the churning noise of the sea, floated toward the *Orion*. As if in response to the eerie signal, the entire school of sharks immediately dove down into the water and disappeared. At once, as if someone had waved a magic wand, the wind died and the roiling ocean began to calm. In the sky above, the storm clouds drifted away, revealing a full moon.

"What magic is this?" Tarik cried out.

"We are saved!" Kalif shouted.

"Think so?" Tragon asked.

"Look," the Assurian said. "The sharks have gone!"

Again the weird cry sounded out in the darkness. The crew waited, peering apprehensively into the night. An involuntary gasp went up from the men. Ahead on the dark water, Tragon saw something coming in their direction. A ship with black sails glided silently across the shimmering dark water. A name appeared on the side of the ship in red letters that seemed to burn with some inner fire: "Chimera." Venora was coming.

3

Tragon's eyes swept the approaching ship's deck, and a shiver ran down his spine, when he spied the vessel's crew. Tattered rags covered skeletal bodies that were only half-covered in flesh. Hollow eyes glowed like burning coals. The ghastly crew of the *Chimera* waited ready to attack, armed with swords, pikes, gaffs, knives and clubs.

On the quarter deck, stood a tall, familiar female figure dressed in black—Venora, Queen of The Dark Island of Dolfar. At her side stood something that was neither man nor ape, but half of each. Gorg, high priest of Dolfar. The mysterious creature held the ship's wheel in one hand, a ram's horn in the other. He raised the horn to his lips. Again the eerie, haunting note they had heard before sounded and resounded over the dark water.

"I should have known there was no escaping her," Tragon said. He looked over at Yusef, who stood gaping in amazement at the ghoulish apparition that floated toward them.

Tragon ordered his men to prepare for battle. He drew his own cutlass from the scabbard hanging from his belt and prepared for the worst. The *Chimera* drifted closer, turning its port side to the *Orion*. Tragon could feel the apprehension of his men as they watched the skeletal crew of the *Chimera* moving fitfully about the deck of their ship, hungry for the attack. The ships touched, grappling hooks flew, and, with ghastly screams, the crew of the black ship swung across on their lines and boarded the *Orion*.

Tragon's men met the assault head on. Blades slashed and hacked, dug deep into moldy flesh, shattered decaying bone. But to no avail. Though cut and wounded the uncanny things moved forward, stabbing with their rapiers, clubbing with their cudgels, tearing flesh with the sharp hooks of the gaffs. Whenever one of Tragon's men began to falter, the gruesome creatures pounced on him, tearing his weapon away, bony fingers encircling his throat.

Tragon saw one creature force his best swordsman, Dak-Bar, down and attempt to tear out the man's throat with his teeth. Tragon sprang toward the attacker and brought the blade of his cutlass down on the back of his neck. Iron sliced through flesh and bone and the creature's head rolled onto the deck. Dak-Bar scrambled away on his back, got on his knees, and bowed before Tragon with his hands clasped in prayer.

"On your feet, Dak-Bar," Tragon said. "There is more killing to be done before this night is over."

Then to their horror, they saw the headless body of the slain Dolfarian rise up from the deck, its sword still in its hand. Dak-Bar screamed in panic. Tragon swung his cutlass and the creature's sword hand separated from his arm. When the sword fell to the deck, Tragon grabbed hold of the ghastly sea-man's half-flesh-covered ribs, picked him up bodily and tossed him overboard.

Dak-Bar, still on his knees, continued salaaming Tragon, bowing his head to the deck. Tragon let out a curse, as more of the Dolfarians moved in on him. Dak-Bar sprang to his feet, blade in hand, to fight at his captain's side. Tragon's blade made a silver blur in the moonlight as he rained blow after blow upon the undead creatures that came at him. The ghoulish pirates' faces were little more than death's head skulls covered with strips of rotting flesh. Tragon sidestepped a lunge from one of the ghastly things and sent his blade in between its ribs, slicing through its spine. The half-skeleton crumpled over, two halves of its body falling to the deck.

Tragon saw Yusef on the starboard side of the *Orion*, surrounded by three of Venora's sailors. The Jadian had tossed his bow aside and now fought with a sword in one hand and a club in the other. Yusef's clanging blade severed an arm. His club came down, splintering a pale skull. The evil thing fell at his feet, yet still more came at him.

Tragon could see Yusef was in no immediate danger, but he knew that the battle on deck was not going well. Too many of his men had fallen, and he shivered in horror at the grisly sight of the Dolfarians feasting on the flesh of his fallen men. Tragon glanced over at the *Chimera* and saw the queen of the dark island still standing on the quarterdeck watching the battle. Gorg stood next to her.

Tragon ran to the bulwark, jumped up on it and grabbed one of the grappling lines the Dolfarians had used to board his ship. Kicking one of the bloodthirsty fiends away he leaped out into space and swung over to the *Chimera*.

4

No sooner did he land on the other ship's deck than half a dozen of the grisly men of the Dark Queen jumped from the *Orion* back onto their own ship and leaped upon him. Tragon fought like a mad man. Two of the attackers went down under his cutlass and then Tragon felt sharp steel pierce his upper arm, as the blade of one of the Dolfarians scored a hit. Tragon fought on but sheer force of numbers was too great. He was soon brought down. He lay on his back, disarmed, looking up at two of the hideous skull-heads. One of them raised his sword to strike the fatal blow, and Tragon prepared himself for death.

"Stop!" A female voice called out. "Do not kill him!" The dark queen had spoken. "Bring him to me." The undead things pulled Tragon to his feet, and marched him toward the quarterdeck. As he approached, Tragon saw Venora, eyes narrowed in rage, glaring down at him from under the black hood she wore. She was as beautiful, in her wicked, perverse way, as she had been when he left her two nights ago, but something about her had changed. Even partially hidden by the hooded cape, her cheeks now seemed hollow and her face appeared noticeably older than before.

"Tragon, how could you have done such a thing?" she asked. The icy imperiousness slipped away from her face. "To me, the woman who loved you more than human words can say."

"Delusions of love were all in your mind, Venora," Tragon said.

"You speak so cruelly to me now," the dark queen said. "What have I done to deserve such treatment at your hands—the hands of the only man I ever loved?"

"You speak of love," Tragon said. "What does a 500 year old witch know of love? What you call love on your terms is only an evil perversion."

"I promised you eternal life, Tragon," she said. "What other woman in this world could offer you that?"

"Eternal life," Tragon said. He looked over at the *Orion* where Venora's monstrous crew were still locked in deadly combat with his men. "Is that what those fiends call it? More like eternal damnation."

"I thought you would stay with me."

"It was only because warships pursued me that I sought safe refuge on Dolfar Island in the first place. Had I known the evil that dwells on Dolfar, I would rather have taken chances with my pursuers. Better to die a pirate than become a living corpse."

"You used charm to convince me to let you live," Venora said. "And you possessed enough charm to make me fall in love with you. But I see now it was all pretense. When I was at my most vulnerable, you seduced me, drugged me with some potion and fled. Two days it has taken to catch up to you. I sent that storm to delay you."

She came down the steps of the quarter deck and the simian-featured Gorg followed her. She stood before Tragon, her eyes suddenly cold and merciless. "And now that I have you, I no longer want you!" she said. Her hand shot out and a resounding slap cracked on the side of Tragon's face. "Where is it? Where is the Red Heart of Dolfar?"

Tragon heard the screams of his men back on the Orion, men dying under the onslaught of her ghoulish crew.

"I thought we would come to that," he said.

"Give it back to me, Tragon. You have no idea of its importance. Where is it?"

"Where neither you nor your men will find it."

"I will tear your ship to shreds."

"It will do you no good. It's in a place that will never be discovered, if you don't know where to look."

Gorg moved forward, a deep growl rumbling up from his chest. "No," the queen commanded in a cold, quiet voice. She looked across the water at the *Orion*, where a blood bath raged.

"Do you see, Tragon? You're men are being slaughtered. Not one of them will live, unless you give me the stone. Turn it over to me now and you and your men will be spared."

"And I'm supposed to take your word on that?"

Venora nodded to Gorg. The ape-man raised the ram's horn to his lips and blew out that single primitive note that Tragon had heard before. As the horn wailed, the crew of the *Chimera* suddenly ceased its attack. Tragon could see his men getting to their feet and backing away from the creatures, who now stood like silent statues.

"Another blast from that horn," Venora said, "And they will return to life and finish what they have started."

Tragon spotted his first mate on the deck of the *Orion*. He called out. "Yusef, are you all right?"

"Aye, captain," the Jadian answered.

"It's your last chance, Tragon," Venora said. "Give me the ruby."

Tragon's mind raced. He knew he could not trust the witch. Yet, he could not risk another attack on his men. He could see how desperate Venora was to get the stone back. Perhaps, he thought, he could use her desperation to buy enough time to find a way out of his predicament.

"Yusef," he shouted. "Bring the Red Heart of Dolfar."

"But, captain---"

"Quickly, Yusef."

5

Yusef strode across the *Orion's* deck, went through a door in the ship's poop, and went down below. Gorg's pig-like eyes watched Tragon carefully. The palm of the ape-man's hairy hand rested on the hilt of the sword that hung from his jewel-encrusted belt. Tragon's bloodied crew stood waiting, not knowing what to expect. A moment later, Yusef appeared back on deck, holding a small wooden box.

"Bring it here," Venora said.

Yusef grabbed one of the grappling lines and swung over to the *Chimera*. He walked up to Tragon and handed him the box.

"Open it," Venora ordered.

Tragon lifted a gold latch that kept the oak lid shut. He opened it. Inside the box lay a huge blood red ruby resting on a black velvet cloth. It gleamed and sparkled in the bright moonlight.

"Take it out, and hand it to me," Venora said.

Tragon lifted the gem from its container. Its smooth glassy surface felt cool to his fingers. It was a marvelous stone, sure to fetch a King's ransom and then some. It would have been a fitting recompense for his sojourn to the Dark Island of Dolfar.

He held out the stone to Venora, who now removed her hooded cape and let it drop to the floor. In the moonlight, Tragon could see indeed had aged considerably since he'd last seen her only two days ago. Her face was lined and wrinkled. Her jet black hair was streaked with grey.

Tragon saw the ornate necklace of gold that hung around her neck. In the center of it was the empty setting from which Tragon had plucked the ruby, before fleeing Dolfar. She took the stone from him and, with trembling fingers, snapped it into place. Immediately, an inner light began to pulsate within the ruby. A reddish glow winked on and off inside the stone, casting its hellish tint over the ship. Every man turned to look at the ruby as its light glowed and faded, glowed and faded.

Tragon's hair stood on end as he suddenly realized that with every pulsating glow of red light, Venora's face became younger. The grey streaks in her hair vanished. In a matter of moments she had become again the beautiful raven-haired women he had first met the day he landed on Dolfar.

"Do you see, Tragon? Am I not beautiful?" she asked. The hatred had disappeared from her eyes. She moved closer. "Do you not regret the way you treated me?"

Tragon remained silent.

"Never in my long life, have I met a man like you," Venora half-whispered. "I saw something in you that first day, when you landed on the beach. Something in your eyes. No man ever captivated me so, with only just a glance." She looked away. "You spurned me. But I know it was only because you feared me. I can forgive you for that, if only now you will tell me that you will come with me back to Dolfar."

She stared at him with the eyes of a jungle cat that hypnotizes its prey before it strikes. Tragon felt himself being drawn to her, despite himself. A strange sensation of listlessness overcame him. Waves of emotion surged, and suddenly, he understood that in her own strange, weird and insane way, the Dark Witch of Dolfar did love him.

"Tragon," Venora said. "Listen to me. You know you want to come back with me. You cannot refuse me. Time will teach you to love me. Say you will come to Dolfar and Gorg will blow the horn and your men will go free."

Her dark eyes became mystic lenses through which he could see a netherworld of eerie beauty. A world that strangely beckoned to him. A world that offered immortality.

Tragon tore his eyes away and glanced over at the men of the *Orion*, who stood watching the scene in rapt fascination.

"If you refuse," Venora said, "your men will all die."

So many lives at stake. With one selfless act, he could save them all. Was it too much to ask? He turned to Yusef.

"Go back to the *Orion,* Yusef. Take our men safely home."

"No, captain--!

"Go. That's an order. Our journey together has come to an end. May you fare well, my friend."

"You cannot let her do this," Yusef said

Tragon looked over at the Chimera. "Too many lives are at stake," Tragon said. "Go now."

Yusef struggled to say something, but, then reached out a hand. The two men clasped each other's forearm.

"Goodbye, my captain."

Yusef walked back down the deck, grabbed the grappling line and swung back on board the *Orion.*

"Call your men off, Venora," Tragon said. "Let's be on our way."

Venora smiled and nodded at Gorg. The ape-man lifted the ram's horn to his lips with both hands to give the signal. Tragon suddenly sprang forward and grabbed the sword from Gorg's scabbard. The high-priest gasped in surprise and Tragon plunged the blade into the high priest's chest. Blood spurted and the creature fell back.

"No!" Venora shrieked. "Again you betray me!"

"You're mad, Venora," Tragon said. "Do you think any man with blood in his veins would want to live with you?" He thrust the sword into her bosom. Venora smiled evilly as Tragon retracted the blade. There was no blood. No wound. Then her smile changed quickly into a snarl of rage.

"You lied to me," she hissed. "All men are liars. No man can be trusted." She waved a hand toward the Dolfarians on board the *Orion.* "Kill them. Kill them all!"

The ghastly beings from Dolfar came back to life and returned to the attack. Tragon plunged his blade deep into Venora's side. Again to no avail.

"Now you will pay for your treachery," the dark queen

sneered.

"There must be a way to stop you," Tragon said. He stood before her, sword in hand, as the stone she wore around her neck, threw its intermittent red light over everything. Then it came to him. He leaped forward, snatched the necklace from her throat, and threw it to the deck.

"No!" Venora screamed.

He knew he had guessed right. He raised the sword above his head and brought it down with all his strength. The sharp edge of the blade struck the red stone in the center. The ruby shattered and there was an explosion of red light. Small fragments of the stone flew in the air above their heads, like red fireflies. Tiny pinpoints of red fire floated up into the night and disappeared. "Tragon!" Venora collapsed against the wall of the quarterdeck, her hand to her breast. Deep lines appeared in her face, thick veins protruded from her neck and forehead. Her arms became as emaciated as the arms of her crewmen and her breath wheezed in her chest. "Tragon!" she cried. "Why? I only wanted to love you. Was that so wrong?"

She held out a hand to him, but the flesh on her fingers dropped to the floor of the deck. "I will be waiting for you," she wheezed. Her withered arm fell to her side and the skin on her face fell away and her head became a hollow skull. All that remained of the Dark Queen of Dolfar collapsed in a gory heap on the floor.

Tragon ran to the *Chimera's* bulwark and saw that all that was left of its crew lay in sickening gobs of flesh and bone on the deck of the *Orion*. He ran for the grappling line to reboard his own ship. As he leaped out into black space, a cold shiver ran down his back as he heard again the dark queen's words: "I will be waiting for you!"

BRIDE OF THE SEA

1

The woman stood naked on the edge of the wooden dock and put the breathing device between her lips. Behind her the gleaming towers of Atlantis rose up into the sky, sparkling in the bright sunshine. Without so much as a glance at the magnificent city at her back, she dove off the dock and plunged into the clear blue water of the ocean. Down she swam, her long dark hair streaming behind her in the water. The water was cool and refreshing after the hot temperature on the surface above. She swam down to the colorful plants and blossoms that lay amidst the sea grass a hundred feet below the surface—down along the bright pink and white coral reefs.

Her body moved in graceful ululations. Rippling motions from shoulders to thighs sent her streaking through the clear blue waters of the Sargasso Sea. The breathing device let her stay under the water as long as she wanted. And after a while, she saw her, rising up from behind the reef, moving fast toward her. Seela, the dolphin sea oracle swam straight to her, then circled around her.

"Nyerie," Seela said, her words unspoken but clearly heard in the woman's mind. "Queen of Atlantis! You come like a bride of the sea. It makes me happy to see you. Happy but also sad."

"Seela," Nyerie answered. She turned a summersault under the water. "Why are you sad? It is a glorious day in the sea and all creatures should be happy."

"Aye, a beautiful day it is," Seela answered. "But one that will bring full measure of tragedy, my Nyerie."

Nyerie froze, her body suspended in the water. The dolphin's words gave substance to the terrible feeling she'd had since awakening that morning. That dark foreboding of something evil coming her way was what made her seek out her sea oracle. "Why do you speak thus?" she asked. "What terrible thing can happen? Am I not queen of the most powerful land on this planet? Are not the marvels we have created such as the world has never seen? Have we not put our resources and talents to use for the good of all? What tragedy can come of this?"

The dolphin swam around her as she floated suspended underwater. "The tragedy that befalls all who dare resist a greater power," she said.

"The Eternal One?" She knew now that her dread was for a reason.

"He comes," Seela said. "I have seen his arrival this day. He has come for a reckoning."

The dolphin's words sent an icy chill down her spine. But then she threw her shoulders back. "And he shall have it," she said. "I do not fear him."

"My Nyerie," Seela said. "My beautiful one. I fear for you. Your beauty is equally matched by your bravery. But against such a one as he, keeper of the law of Zarkon, how can you stand against him?"

"I made my decision to oppose his cruel dictates. I am prepared to face the consequences." She looked up toward the surface. "Surely those on the side of right and justice must prevail in this world."

"This world does not care about right or justice," Seela said. "Those are only human concepts. This is a world that destroys and devours all who live on it, just as they destroy and devour one another. Human concepts count for nothing."

"I must go, Seela," Nyerie said. The dolphin's words made her angry. "I must prepare. Thank you for your pre-sight. You are a good friend. But I don't believe in your view of the world. I can never believe in a world that cruel."

She swam up toward the surface.

"Farewell, Nyerie," Seela called after her. "May the sea gods protect you."

2

Back on the dock, Nyerie threw her white tunic on and tied a gold-braided belt around her waist. She had to get back to the palace and tell Banseer, her husband and co-ruler of Atlantis, what the dolphin had told her. She had to find her son, Tarka, and put him in safe keeping. She walked quickly to her Sky-bike parked a few feet away and swung into the saddle. A twist of the handlebar and the anti-grav motor engaged.

The bike rose up off the dock and ascended rapidly. High in the air, the fantastic city spread out below her. Atlantis was built in three concentric rings, each ring separated by water. The outer ring, from which she'd just arisen, was the industrial and waterfront area. Great ships were moored along the edge of the sea, and giant warehouses, where the grains and foodstuffs that came from cities around the globe, stood along the waterfront. On the inland side of the outer ring were the great airports where flying machines of all sizes and shapes took off and landed on domestic and trans-oceanic flights.

She passed over the waterway that separated the third ring from the second, scarcely noticing, her mind intent on what she knew she had to do. On the second ring were the homes of the general populace of Atlantis. Here lived workers and professionals of every stripe. There were no poor and no rich on Atlantis, only a wide-based middle class that lived together in homes that were comfortable and suitable to their means.

Crossing over the second waterway, she flew over the Central Hub, the heart of Atlantis, where her palace stood, where the Hall of Science and the House of Fine Arts and the Arena of Games were located. Behind the palace, and towering over it all, rose the peak of a volcano. A blue spiral of smoke curled up from the mouth of Mt. Mord, and trailed in the sky high above the palace's north tower. Despite the smoke, the lava in the dormant volcano's fiery bowels had lain quiet and undisturbed for centuries.

Nyerie flew toward the palace, and cast an apprehensive glance at the strangely stunted pyramid that stood on the other side of a wide avenue—the Temple of Zarkon. The pyramid, made of granite, rose up a hundred feet, but instead of culminating in a sharp point, stopped three quarters of the way up, as if its upper third had been cut off, leaving a wide, flat surface at the top. She knew too well what that flat level surface was for, and she shuddered.

She circled around to the western façade of the palace. The sky-bike touched down on the flag-stone floor of the landing terrace and Nyerie ran past the attendants who came out to greet her. She raced through a large, ornately furnished room, through massive oak doors and down a long hallway. She heard the clang of steel behind another door along the hall and entered that room. Banseer, her husband, a tall, broad-shouldered man, and Tarka, her son of nine, stood in the center of the room with swords crossed.

"Mommy," Tarka yelled. "Watch!" The boy turned to his father and lunged forward with his sword. Banseer stepped back and parried his son's sword, whereupon Tarka began a ferocious series of strikes, his smaller sword sending up sparks as it hit his father's stout blade. The man stepped further and further back. Finally Banseer was backed against a marble pillar and could not move.

"See, mommy," Tarka yelled. "I've got father pinned!"

"Very good, son," Banseer said. He slid his blade down along the boy's sword and diverted it down to the floor. "But when you have a man cornered, you must not hesitate to follow through." With a twist of his wrist, the boy's sword flew in the air over his head. Banseer caught it. "It is not the time for conversation."

"Aww!" Tarka said, as his father tossed the sword back to him. "I know that. I just wanted to show mommy." He ran to her.

"Banseer," Nyerie said. "We must talk." She kissed the boy. "Tarka, it is time for your music lesson."

"I hate music," the boy said. "I hate old Klystrono. He makes me play the same scales over and over."

"Go!" Nyerie ordered. "And when you're done I want you to bring your *rebat*. I want to hear what you've learned."

"All right," the boy said, clomping out of the room, his head bowed in dejection.

Banseer came to her and kissed her. "What is it? You seem anxious."

"They are coming," she said, her eyes wide with fear. "I knew this day would come and thought I was prepared for it. Now I'm afraid."

"How do you know?"

"Seela told me. Something told me I should seek my sea-oracle today. Her visions of the future are never wrong."

"Your ability to hear the thoughts of that creature astounded me at first. Only you have that gift. But her predictions have been too accurate in the past for me to doubt now. What do we do? Do you still plan to resist the Law of Zarkon?"

"With every atom of my being," Nyerie said. "I have gone too far to change course now.

"You know the penalty," Banseer said. "The Eternal One will bring powerful weapons when he comes."

"Yes, I know the penalty," Nyerie said. "But I also know that the long reign of Lien, the Eternal One, the keeper of the Law of Zarkon, must end. I have created a new vision for our people, as my mother wished. A new way of life. We can no longer carry out the cruel, self-serving demands of the Law of Zarkon."

She stepped free of Banseer's embrace and walked toward a window that overlooked the skyline of Atlantis. Gleaming spires rose up into the bright blue sky and down in the streets below moved the citizens of the most advanced city in the ancient world. Banseer came up behind her and put his hands on her shoulders and gazed out at the city with her.

"A thousand years ago," Nyerie said, "Lien, the Eternal One, came to this planet from Zarkon and left our ancient ancestors the machines and equipment and the knowledge to build this magnificent city. In return, for a thousand years, our people fulfilled the Law of Zarkon. They built Atlantis and then with sheer dominance of technology conquered the kingdoms of Earth. They destroyed the city of pyramids and made slaves of the people, took their jewels and brought them back here in their flying machines and sailing ships. They conquered the lands to the east and brought more slaves and fine jade and rare silks. They invaded the lands of ice and snow and brought the furs and skins of the snow beasts. All these things they brought here so that when Lien, the Eternal One, came, they could give them to him as tribute.

"Every hundred years, the Eternal One comes and collects his tribute. He takes his slaves and his jewels and his riches back to Zarkon. For ten centuries Atlantis has existed only to serve him. And now he comes again. But this time he will find no tribute." She turned to Banseer and looked up into his cool, grey eyes. "Yes, he has powerful weapons," she said. "But we have weapons of our own. When I decided to break the Law of Zarkon, I knew what we would face, and I instructed Jankar to create a weapon in his laboratory powerful enough to destroy Lien, if need be. He has completed development of it just in time."

Banseer took her in his arms and she looked up into his eyes. She could see the love he held for her, and, perhaps, a little fear there as well. "My love, my queen," he said. "What you have decided is what should be. It is the right thing. I will support you. Just as our people have expressed their support. We are all behind you. And if it proves necessary, I will fire Jankar's weapon."

He held her closer to him and she felt his heart beating in his chest.

"And I know it will be necessary," he said. "Lien will not leave without either his tribute or his revenge."

3

It was noon when the ship from Zarkon appeared in the sky over Atlantis. It gleamed in the bright Atlantean sunlight, hovering over the central hub of the city---a triangular-shaped object made of shiny steel. The people of Atlantis ran from their homes. They poured into the streets and over the bridges that spanned the waterways. They pointed in fear and awe at the massive thing hovering above them.

Nyerie stood with Banseer and another man on the balcony outside her throne room and watched as the craft descended from the sky. Suddenly a loud, frightening blast of sound came from the ship—like the sound of a thousand ram's horns. The people in the streets cried out in fear. Nyerie watched in nervous anticipation as the ship moved laterally and came closer to the palace. There was another ominous blast from the ship and it stopped its lateral movement. It was now positioned directly above the stunted pyramid that stood opposite the palace. Nyerie gripped Banseer's hand tightly as another blast sounded and the ship lowered itself down toward the Temple of Zarkon.

The craft came down slowly, then Nyerie heard the crunch and grind of metal and stone as the ship settled down on top of the temple, its shape and form perfectly completing the top of the temple's pyramid design. There was a final blast from the ship's horn and then silence.

"Is all in readiness?" Nyerie asked, turning to the man standing next to her husband. He was an older man with grey hair and beard.

"Yes, your majesty," he said, bowing. "The weapon is ready and mounted on the Northern tower. The western portion of the city has been evacuated."

"Good work, Jankar," Nyerie said. "If we succeed, it will be in no small measure due to your efforts."

The man bowed again.

She turned to Banseer. "Is Tarka safe?"

"Yes," Banseer answered. "He has his servants and three guards."

"Good," Nyerie said. "I go now to greet our visitors. When I give the signal, fire the weapon. Hopefully, a demonstration of its power will be enough."

"Jankar has instructed me in its use," Banseer said. "And if a demonstration is insufficient to convince the Eternal One, I know what to do."

She embraced Banseer. "May it go well," she said. "May I return to you and Tarka, and may Atlantis at last be free."

4

Nyerie strode down the palace steps surrounded by ten armed soldiers, each clad in armor and equipped with ray-beam rifles. In the bright blue sky above her, she could see the pale blue smoke that drifted over the palace from the mouth of Mt. Mord. With her escort she crossed the boulevard, the crowd in the street parting to let her pass, and proceeded up the steps of the Temple of Zarkon. Nyerie could feel the heat of the sun rising up from the stone steps of the pyramid. She could hear the murmur of the crowd behind her, watching fearfully, not knowing what to expect.

They knew the Law of Zarkon. They knew of Lien, the Eternal One. No one living had ever seen him, but they knew the history. They'd read the story and seen the pictures of Lien painted by artists of past generations. They knew of Nyerie's decision to set Atlantis free from the Law of Zarkon. She had spoken at the Assembly Hall and the majority had voted to support her. There were those who opposed her, because they were afraid of the consequences, but their fears were silenced by Nyerie's eloquent speech and the fervor of the majority. Atlantis must be free!

Halfway up the temple steps, Nyerie heard a strange whirring noise and the steel doors of the Zarkon ship slid open. Nyerie stopped. For a moment there was only blackness behind the doors. Then something bright yellow appeared in the doorway. It was tall and long and moved forward into the daylight. Nyerie's resolve almost disintegrated when she saw the being standing there at the top of the steps. The creature was fully eight feet tall, wrapped in bright yellow silk. Its head was elongated and its skin was dark red, like a sea-lobster. Large yellow eyes with flabby, drooping lids that half-covered them, gazed down at her. They were eyes thousands of years old and they looked at her as if she were nothing more than a fly. The eyes darted suspiciously from her to the armed men that stood on either side of her.

Lien, the Eternal One, came down the temple steps slowly and as he did, armed soldiers followed him out of the ship. They were strange-looking beings, obviously not of the same race as the Eternal One. They were short, mishapen creatures carrying rifles of their own. Twenty of them marched out of the ship behind Lien.

Lien descended half the distance to Nyerie and came to a halt. His long head turned from side to side, taking in the crowds of people in the streets below and then his blood shot eyes finally came to rest on Nyerie again.

"You are Nyerie?" he asked. His voice was dry and hollow sounding, like a voice calling up from an ancient tomb. "Granddaughter of Rakma, the maid-servant who served me so well when last I came?"

"Yes, I am Nyerie, granddaughter of Rakma, *Queen* of Atlantis," Nyerie said, emphasizing the word "queen" strongly.

The thing from Zarkon looked down at her with disdain. "And is this how the granddaughter of my maid-servant greets me? With armed guards?" He looked down at the crowds. "Why are the people so silent? Why are they not singing in joy at my arrival as did crowds in the past? Where are my slaves, lying on the temple steps for me to walk on rather than these bare, hot stones? What has happened in this far-flung colony? Have I been away too long? Has Atlantis forgotten how to treat its God?"

"Atlantis has changed, Lien," Nyerie said. "There are no slaves for you. There is no tribute. No jewels nor gold. Only a warning. Leave Atlantis and never come back."

There was dead silence for a moment as the Eternal One stared down at her in disbelief. Then Nyerie heard a dry, clicking sound, like a twig scraping on a rock, and realized it was Lien cackling to himself. "Do you wish to die?" he asked. "Would you like to see your people destroyed?"

"No," Nyerie answered. She nodded her head and her armed escort raised their weapons and pointed them at the thing standing above them. "They call you the Eternal One," she said. "But I wonder what will happen if one of my soldiers sends a ray beam through those pretty silken robes?"

Lien let out a hiss of outrage and raised one clawed hand. The soldiers behind him raised their weapons and a bright beam of white light shot out from one of the soldiers rifles. The guard at Nyerie's right hand screamed and fell. He lay still, a black hole smoking in the center of his armored chest.

"Hold!" Lien shrieked. "I gave no order to fire."

The soldiers on both sides crouched and waited, fingers tight on triggers. Lien's guards looked at him in confusion. Nyerie could see the blood lust rising in their savage eyes. She raised a cautionary hand to her own men.

"You are wise to hold," Nyerie said. She turned and pointed up behind her to the palace's north tower. "My husband is ready to destroy you, your ship and all aboard it." She watched as Lien's eyes moved up along the front of the palace. His eyes blazed an even brighter yellow when he saw the huge canon mounted on the tower. It was fully twenty feet long, its barrel made of alternating panels of steel and some transparent material, through which the pulsating glow of white energy shone brightly even in broad daylight.

"Atlantis is newly dedicated to the causes of peace and compassion," Nyerie said. "We have foresworn the evil ways of our past. No longer will we conquer and destroy other lands to serve your greedy desire for tribute. No longer will we make war on people struggling to create their own civilizations so that we may turn them into slaves to serve you. No longer do we obey the Law of Zarkon!"

Lien lowered his eyes from the cannon and looked down at her. Nyerie wanted to look away from the evil and the hate that was in those eyes, but she held her gaze.

"Those who disobey the Law of Zarkon can know only one outcome," the Eternal One said. "Think twice before committing you and all your people to the fate to which you are condemning them."

"We have all agreed," Nyerie said. "Atlantis is a free city, now. All are free to speak their minds. It has been decided."

"Has it now?" Lien asked. He looked past her down to the crowd below. "People of Atlantis," he hollered. "Does your queen speak for all of you? Are you all so brave that you would willingly defy the Law of Zarkon and face the supreme penalty?"

The crowd hesitated.

"Speak up, citizens of Atlantis," Nyerie yelled. "Do you want to remain slaves of Zarkon or would you be free? Slavery or freedom. Which will it be?"

"Freedom!" one man shouted out. "Freedom," another repeated. Soon other cried out and then another. In a moment a chant arose from the crowd. "Free-dom. Free-dom."

"No, no!" a woman yelled. "We must obey the Law of Zarkon, as we always have. I do not want to die."

Several others shouted their opposition to Nyerie's position. Those who supported Nyerie tried to out shout them.

Lien raised his long arms and the crowd became silent.

"There seems to be a lack of unanimity," he said.

"Don't be afraid, citizens," Nyerie shouted. "We have the upper hand. Your good king Banseer stands behind us with a weapon more powerful than anything known on Zarkon."

"How do we know the weapon is as powerful as you say it is?" a doubter in the crowd asked.

"I knew there would be need for a demonstration," Nyerie said. "We have prepared. The western section of Central Atlantis, our former military headquarters, has been evacuated. What you are about to see should convince you."

She turned and looked up at Banseer and raised her arm. Banseer swung the long barrel of the cannon to the west. He took only a second to aim and a bright red beam of light shot out of the cannon's mouth. Half a dozen buildings in the evacuated part of the city turned bright red and then simply crumbled to the ground.

A cry of awe went up from the crowd. Banseer turned the cannon back and aimed it at Lien, his soldiers and the Zarkon ship behind them.

"One blast, Eternal One," Nyerie said, "And you will vanish like those buildings."

"A costly demonstration," Lien said.

"What was destroyed can be easily rebuilt and put to better purposes. We have no need for such a large military installation. Renouncing imperialism in the name of peace and compassion, we have need for only a small, efficient security force."

"How very idealistic," Lien said, sarcastically.

"Call it what you will," Nyerie said. "This change in our national destiny was the wish of my mother, Queen Tirzaa and I am carrying out her wishes. Already we have signed peace treaties with the people of the pyramid country, and are giving them the technology to rebuild their civilization. They will become one of the most powerful kingdoms this world has ever seen. We have done the same with the yellow skinned countries and the people of black skin. With the technology formerly used to destroy and conquer we are building a new world, such as no one has ever seen."

Silence followed Nyerie's speech. The crowd stood waiting. Above them Banseer stood ready behind the cannon. Then that dry cackling laugh rose up again from the Eternal One's thin, withered chest.

"You would have done better to have that cannon pointed here," Lien said.

"We have pledged our lives to giving life not taking it," Nyerie said. "We will not kill you, if you leave now and never return."

The Eternal One's yellow eyes looked down on her coldly, and the withered red skin on his face cracked as his lips sneered.

"We will go, Nyerie," he said. "Enjoy your few moments of freedom."

A shudder ran down Nyerie's spine at those words. The long, yellow-robed figure turned and ascended the steps. Should she give the order to Banseer to fire? What did Lien mean? The last few minutes of freedom. Was it an empty threat, or would he try something?

She thought of Tarka, hidden safely in a secret chamber of the palace with his hand servants. Could she risk his precious life on the chance that the Eternal One would not try to harm Atlantis before he left? All she had to do was raise her hand and Banseer would fire. But to do so would be to sacrifice her principles. She had changed the course of history on the basis of a commitment to peace and compassion. Cold bloodedly killing Lien could not be justified. No, she would wait and see. Only if Lien made a move, would she give the order.

She waited breathlessly as the elongated figure climbed the last step and entered the darkened portal of the ship. Lien's soldiers backed in through the doorway, their weapons trained on Nyerie, Banseer and the crowd below. Finally the steel door shut and, through the stone steps beneath her feet, Nyerie felt the vibration of the ship's motor as it thrummed to life.

"Come," she said, turning to her escort. They flew down the steps, nearly falling in the pell-mell rush. Finally they made it to the street. She heard a deep rumbling sound and then the frightening blast of the ship's horn. Screams rose up from the crowd and people began backing away from the temple. The Temple of Zarkon trembled and shook and then the ship lifted off from its base. It rose up a hundred feet or more and Nyerie held her breath. She looked over her shoulder and saw Banseer pointing the canon up at the ship. Something inside told her she should have let Banseer kill the Eternal One before he got back into his ship. It was foolhardy to believe he would just leave without retaliation. But she knew Banseer would fire at the first sign of something amiss.

Then, to her horror, she saw a yellow ray of light shoot out from the front of the Eternal One's ship. At the same moment the red ray emitted from Banseer's cannon. The beams passed each other and the top of the palace and the ship exploded at the same time.

Nyerie felt her heart shrivel. Half of the North tower was gone. She looked skyward. The triangular ship was badly damaged. It careened wildly in circles several hundred feet above the city. Yellow ray beams sprayed out of it, landing promiscuously amidst different parts of the city. Buildings exploded and walls fell. The crowd stampeded in blind panic. The ship was headed for the ocean, but Lien was taking as much revenge as he could before his own end came

"Tarka!" Nyerie screamed. She ran across the boulevard and up the palace steps. As she approached the entrance she looked back and saw the Eternal One's disintegrating ship fire one last shot. The bright yellow ray ran high above her and she heard it hit something behind the palace. Then the ship wobbled over on its side and plunged into the ocean beyond Atlantis's third outer ring, a cloud of white smoke trailing behind it. At least, she thought, the Eternal One was no more.

She ran into the palace, through the main hall and up a flight of marble steps. Down a long corridor she found the chamber where Tarka had been hidden. She threw the door open and saw her son standing next to the two women and the three armed guards who had kept him under their protection.

"Did you see that, mommy," he shouted, running to her. "Did you see the ship fall into the ocean? Father got him."

"Yes, my son," Nyerie said, scooping the boy up in her arms. "I saw it." She hugged the boy tightly.

"Where is father," Tarka asked. "Is he coming?"

Nyerie was afraid to tell her son what she feared had happened to Banseer. There was a commotion at the door. Nyerie turned. Banseer stood in the doorway, covered in dust and blood.

"Banseer!" Nyerie ran to him. "You're alive!"

Banseer embraced her. "Yes, but Jankar was not so lucky."

"I should have let you kill Lien with the first shot. I was a fool to think we could escape his wrath that easily"

"Some of the city has been destroyed," Banseer said. "But we can easily rebuild it. The most important thing is that we are all alive and that evil thing has been destroyed. Do you realize what that means? You've changed the fate of this world, beloved. Now Atlantis can truly be a force for peace and progress on this Earth. It is the beginning of a new era."

Suddenly the floor beneath their feet shook. A deep rumbling came up from the earth beneath the palace. A deafening explosion came from the rear of the building.

"What's that, mommy?" Tarka asked.

Nyerie looked into Banseer's eyes and at that moment both knew what it was.

"Come," Banseer said. They ran out of the chamber, down another hallway to the other side of the palace. They entered a room on the West side and ran to the window. Nyerie saw hot molten lava pouring through a wide fissure in the side of Mt. Mord.

There was another explosion and a fireball flew out of the top of the volcano and landed in the middle of the public square on the south side of the palace. Dozens of people were crushed and burned. Hundreds ran screaming for their lives.

"It was Lien's final shot," Nyerie said. "It must have hit Mt. Mord and broken it apart. The Eternal One will have his revenge on us after all."

The three of them stood together holding each other watching as the top of the mountain blew off and was hurled high into the air. Flames and lava belched out of the broken mountain and a river of flaming red magma began rolling toward them. Again the earth shook and rumbled as a deep fissure split the ground in two from the volcano to the palace. "It was all for nothing," Nyerie said. Banseer held her and their child tighter. She thought of Seela's words.

"This world does not care about right or justice," Seela had said. "Those are only human concepts. This is a world that destroys and devours all who live on it, just as they destroy and devour one another. Human concepts count for nothing."

Outside the palace a scene of pandemonium and mad panic ensued, as the crowd ran across the bridges and dove into the waterways separating the rings of Atlantis. Walls and columns toppled, buildings flattened and became cracked slabs of stone. Only half of the crowd managed to escape to the second ring before they heard a horrendous explosion and a sound like the Earth itself cracking in half. They turned and stood watching in rapt horror as the palace and most of Central Atlantis suddenly shuddered and heaved upward and then fell down into the sea. Screaming in sheer terror they ran toward the last outer ring where the ships and aircraft waited. If they could only get to them on time.

But before a single ship could be launched or aircraft lifted from a runway, the rings of Atlantis cracked and crumbled. Giant tidal waves rolled in from the ocean and crushed anything that still remained, and, in a matter of hours, all that was left of the once great civilization were the trembling air bubbles that floated on the surface of the water.

5

Long strands of seaweed and kelp dance and weave themselves around the broken stones and cracked walls of an ancient palace that stands at the bottom of the sea. Crabs crawl along the tilted walls, schools of fish dart in and out of the empty windows. From a distance a dolphin could be seen swimming up from behind a coral reef. She swims around the once mighty parapets of the castle and circles curiously about the shattered tower that once topped the north side of the building. The dolphin skates along the algae-covered façade of the palace as though it were looking for something. Finally she dives to the bottom and turns to look up at the once magnificent structure.

"Nyerie!" The dolphin calls. "It is Seela, my beautiful one. Where have you gone? It was as I said it would be, was it not? Oh, my Nyerie. So beautiful you were, but even more beautiful was your heart. So full of noble ideas. You tried to make a better world. You wanted to destroy an evil thing. You succeeded, my beautiful queen. But at such a price. You lie here now forever, truly a bride of the sea."

The dolphin moves along the front of the palace. "I will miss you, Nyerie. Nevermore shall we swim and talk together. The people who come after you will never know what you did for them. They will say you were only a myth, if they remember you at all. It is the way of the world. It devours everything."

The dolphin starts to turn her back on the ruins of Atlantis, then stops. She looks one last time at the sunken palace in the misty blue water. "But still, while you lived you fought for something you believed in—something good and pure and true, and there is nobility in that. You may have been defeated, but your spirit will live on in those yet to come who never knew you but who have the same hunger for freedom. There is victory in that."

With a flick of her tail fin she turns and swims away.

" . . WHERE THERE BE NO DRAGONS. . ."

1

Regvald stood there unable to move. Unable to speak. The smell of burning wood filled his nostrils. The humble structure that he had lived in half his life now lay in charred ruin. The clay walls and wooden beams now were all black and broken, crumbling on the ground—barely recognizable. Smoke burned his eyes, but the tears rolling down his cheeks and bearded jowls did not come from the blue wisps and plumes that rose up from what was left of his home. He stepped into the ruin and pushed a black, broken beam aside. Amidst the burnt wreckage he could see charcoaled pieces of bone. An anguished cry tore from his lips and he sank to his knees with a sob. Then he saw something else. A silver amulet lay in the ashes amidst the still warm bones. It was seared black by the fire, but the engraving of the bull that was his family emblem was still plainly visible. He picked the medallion up and did not feel the hot silver burning the flesh in the palm of his hand. He simply knelt there and stared at it in silence.

"It was the Dragon from the Black Mountain," a voice said.

Regvald looked up. A short, blond-headed young man who was called Kelf stood outside the perimeter of the burnt ruin. He was dressed in a simple brown tunic and leggings.

"I saw him with my own eyes," Kelf said. "There's no

mistaking him. He came down from his mountain lair in broad daylight and attacked with no warning. The village didn't have a chance. Look at it!"

Regvald stood up. His gaze swept out past the young villager to the burnt out piles of wreckage and ruin that had once been the village of Hafnil. There was not a building or a hut left standing. All about lay bodies, some burnt beyond recognition. Men and women wondered about the scene as if in a daze. A little girl sat on the ground alone crying.

"If the wall of my hut hadn't fallen over on me, and buried me, I'd be dead like the others," Kelf said. "He knocked my home over with one of his wings, and it was only sheer luck he didn't turn his fiery breath on it or I'd have been fried to a crisp. I was taking a nap when it happened. At first I thought it was an earthquake, but after a minute I came to my senses. I managed to crawl out from under the wall and I saw the monster laying waste to everything."

Regvald said nothing. The tears were gone now. There would be no more tears. His face had the passive expression of a stone mask

"But what no one can understand," Kelf said, "Is why? Why did the dragon attack us? He was like a demon bent on mad destruction. What happened for him to break his pact with us?"

Regvald's face remained as if made of stone as he half-listened to his prattling young friend.

"We've kept our end of the bargain," Kelf said. "I am only a poor farmer. Not a hunter like you. Perhaps it is something beyond my ability to comprehend. For seven years now, since the Dragon came to live on the Black Mountain, we have kept our agreement and he has kept his. We offered him a sacrifice at every Dark Moon, and in return he has kept his promise not to destroy us. What caused him to break the agreement in such a terrible way?"

"Two virgins a year," Regvald said with an angry snarl. "That was the price he extracted from us for our lives. And we were willing to pay it. That was our mistake."

He dropped the amulet into the pocket his wife had sewn

in the side of his leather jerkin and stooped down. He turned his shield over and laid it on the ground. Using it like a tray, he piled his loved ones' bones on it.

2

Regvald threw the last bit of earth over the grave he'd dug and stood up. They were a short distance from the village on a patch of green grass under a tree. He looked out past the grave, across the valley floor and up at the Black Mountain in the grey distance.

"What will you do?" Kelf asked.

"Kill him," Regvald said.

"You *can't* kill him. Nobody can kill a thing like that. It takes a Dragon Slayer. You're a good hunter, but have you ever killed a dragon?"

Regvald's face turned away from the mountain and stared at Kelf. His face was still the same blank mask, but Kelf saw something in the hunter's eyes. Something he had never seen there before. And it frightened him.

Regvald picked up his shield and slung it over his shoulder He took up the scabbarded sword that he had leaned against the tree and belted it around his waist. He grabbed a quiver of arrows and a bow that lay in the grass.

"Let me go with you," Kelf said.

"You're a farmer's son. You must want to die."

"No more than you."

The icy look Regvald gave him sent shivers down Kelf's spine.

"How many daughters did we sacrifice?" Regvald asked. "Fourteen. That's how many since the dragon came to the Black Mountain. One for every Dark Moon. Two times a year when the moon disappears. What did we think we were buying with their lives?"

"It was what the elders decided."

"Why didn't the old fools offer themselves? It seems those with the least to lose are the ones most unwilling to lose it."

"You should have been glad," Kelf said. "You had no

daughters. Only sons."

"And now they're dead too. And so are the elders. The Black Mountain Dragon will pay."

3

They stood on the edge of the mountain pass looking down into the valley. The tree line lay half a kilometer below them. Where they stood, and all the distance to the top, was sheer black granite. A cliff dropped below them several hundred meters. Even from this high up they could still see the blue smoke rising from Hafnil. The wind whistled and Regvald's long brown hair flew in the cold air. The temperature was at least twenty degrees cooler here than down below. The leather jerkin and pants that Regvald's wife had made from the hide of a deer and the cotton shirt she had woven for him kept him warm. Kelf wrapped a dark brown cloak tighter around his shoulders, and shifted the strap of the big water sack he'd brought along.

"Why do dragons have to live so high up?" he asked.

"So they can look down and see all they have dominion over," Regvald said. "And exult in the power they wield."

"I suppose that's good enough reason," the farmer said. "If I had that kind of power, the power of life and death, I suppose that's what I would do."

Regvald gazed down at Hafnil. What had once been a picturesque village nestled among the rolling green hills of the valley was now nothing but a black smudge.

"Look," he said, pointing. "Look how small it seems from here. The world is big, Kelf, and people so small."

They heard the sounds of someone coming toward them from the bend in the pass up ahead. There was nowhere to duck out of sight, so Regvald stood where he was and watched as four dark horsemen came around the turn. They were dressed in black, with black feathers in their hair.

They came single file. The man in the lead seemed big for a Kailoon, who were short, stocky people. A long scar ran down the side of his yellow face. His narrow, slanted eyes glared suspiciously at the two men standing in the middle of the trail. The pass widened out where Regvald and Kelf waited, and the horsemen pulled their mounts up next to each other and stopped a few feet away. The mountain wind whistled eerily as the men eyeballed each other.

"Do you have any money?" the leader said.

"No," Regvald replied.

"You must have something. If you give me something, we will let you live."

"I have this," Regvald said. He reached into his pocket and pulled out the amulet with the bull engraved on it.

The leader got down off his horse. The others followed suit.

"What is that?" the leader said coming toward Regvald.

"It is my family emblem," Regvald said holding it up. He closed his fist around it. "But you can't have it."

The leader stopped a foot away from him. The other three came up next to him. Their eyes darted back and forth between Regvald and Kelf, who stood beside, but a little behind, the hunter.

"Let me see it," the leader said, holding out his left hand. His right hand rested on the hilt of the sword hanging by his side. "You might as well give it to me. We are four against two and one of you isn't even armed. We are up here alone. No one to see what happens. No one to care who lives or dies. Only just this cold mountain. Give it to me."

"Four against one, usually the four gets what it wants," Regvald said. "That's the way of this world. Isn't it? You're Kailoon bandits. You're on your way to raid Hafnil. You've done it before. The strong preying on the weak."

The leader's face clouded over as he listened to Regvald. He didn't like this villager's attitude. He didn't seem scared. And he talked too much. He watched as the man dropped the amulet back in his pocket. He started to lower the hand he'd been holding out. But before he could, Regvald's sword came out of its scabbard and the Kailoon leader stared in shock at the bloody stump at the end of his arm. He screamed in pain and fumbled for his own sword with his left hand. Before it cleared the scabbard, the point of Regvald's blade pierced his chest.

The three other Kailoons drew their weapons as their leader fell. Regvald was on them with the fury of a mad wolf. His blade swung in a shiny blur, as he hacked at the bandits who seemed to be able to do little but try to hold him off. The fury of the Hafnilite's attack stunned them. They were used to the cowardly obeisance that most villagers displayed when they rode up on them. This savage response was something they had never seen before.

But the Kailoons soon recovered from their surprise and after Regvald slashed one of them in the leg they backed off a little. They circled around him warily. Regvald crouched low, his blade held out in front. He sprang at the one nearest the edge of the cliff. The bandit parried his first thrust, but the force of Regvald's attack knocked him off balance. Regvald pushed him back with his sword and the Kailoon's arms shot out sideways as he tried to keep from falling backward over the cliff. Regvald plunged the point of his sword into the bandit's chest . With a scream, the Kailoon fell over the edge of the cliff.

Without pause, Regvald turned and slashed at the nearest of the two remaining bandits. But these fellows were not to be taken so easily. With savage grunts and curses the first one parried his attack and counterattacked with the seasoned skill of a man with years of fighting experience. Regvald was forced back as the man bore down on him. The second Kailoon fell in beside his companion and now Regvald had two blades to contend with. Stepping further back from the attack, his foot came down on a loose rock lying in the middle of the pass. His ankle twisted under him, and pain flared. The Kailoon's blade swung and knocked his sword from his hand as he fell backward. He landed on his back and arrows fell out of his quiver on the ground around him. He regretted now that he had not just shot them all with his bow as they came around the bend.

The Kailoon's eyes lit up as he dove on top of him. He straddled Regvald and lifted his sword up over his chest with both hands on the hilt. Regvald felt the shaft of one of his arrows on the ground under his left hand. He grabbed it and with a savage thrust, plunged the razor sharp arrowhead up into the bandit's throat. The Kailoon gurgled as blood spurted from his jugular. He dropped his sword and clutched at his gushing wound, his fingers turning bright red. Regvald threw the bandit off and started to get up, but the second bandit came running at him, sword at the ready.

The Kailoon stopped suddenly, his body jerked, and he screamed. The bandit fell to the ground. Regvald saw Kelf standing behind him. One of the other Kailoon's swords protruded from the bandit's shoulder blades. Kelf stood wide-eyed, gaping at the man he'd killed.

Regvald tried to get up. Excruciating pain radiated from his ankle and up his leg when he attempted to stand.

"Give me a hand," he told Kelf.

The young farmer was still staring in disbelief at what he'd done.

"I killed him," he said. "He was a savage, murdering Kailoon, the plague of the Steppes, and I killed him. I wouldn't have thought it possible."

"I said give me a hand," Regvald barked.

Kelf snapped out of it and ran to assist the hunter.

"You're hurt," he said, putting his shoulder under Regvald's arm.

"I don't' think it's broken," Regvald said. "Come on. Find some wood to make a splint."

Kelf walked back along the trail looking for wood, glancing back more than once at the man he'd killed.

4

"It's already swelling," Kelf said. He tightened a leather thong around two flat strips of wood that he had placed on either side of Regvald's ankle. "I don't think you broke it. That's the best I can do."

Regvald stood up. He tested the foot gingerly. Sharp pain shot up his leg, but not as bad as before. "It'll do," he said. He started to walk back up the trail.

"Wait," Kelf said. "Let's rest a moment."

"We've wasted enough time."

"We've been walking for hours, and that fight has tired me."

Regvald gave him a sullen glance and shrugged. He sat down on a large rock. Kelf pulled the stopper out of his big water sack and passed it to Regvald. The hunter motioned for him to take the first drink. The farmer sat down on the ground and lifted the sack to his parched lips.

"Why do you carry such a large water sack?" Regvald asked.

"It was my father's," Kelf said. "He was a big man and always thirsty." He made the sign of the cross. "Thank God he never lived to see this day."

"You have no family now?" Regvald asked.

"No," the farmer said. "I've lived alone since my father died." Kelf wiped the dripping water from his chin and passed the goatskin to Regvald. "I'm sorry about your wife and sons," he said. "I was sorry too when I heard what happened to your sister last Dark Moon."

Regvald held the water bag but didn't drink.

"She obeyed the law of the elders," he said. "It was her turn to turn over her daughter to the Dragon. She led Sylvana to the Rocks of Sacrifice and kissed her goodbye. And she left her there to wait for the thing to come in the night and take her. Then my sister came back to her home and hanged herself from the tree next to her house."

"It must have been terrible."

"We thought we had a good arrangement," Regvald said. "All we had to do was sacrifice two virgins a year to save ourselves. We didn't like it, but it was a price we were willing to pay. We told ourselves it was necessary. Something we could live with. A necessary accommodation. But when my sister killed herself, I asked myself *why* did we have to live this way? Why did we make this contract with evil? Why didn't we fight it? Instead of appeasing it." He threw a sharp glance at Kelf. "Who is more to blame? He who commits evil, or he who strikes a bargain with it?"

"We were afraid," Kelf said.

"People are cowards. They're afraid of death, so they live in shame."

"I thought I was about to die back there," Kelf said. "When I saw those four bandits coming around the bend. I thought we would never get away alive."

"How does it feel to kill your first man?" Regvald asked.

Kelf's hand dropped to touch the hilt of the dead man's sword that he now wore on his belt.

"I don't know," he said. "I had no choice. I could not let them kill you."

Regvald nodded. He could see the farmer held himself differently now. He said nothing and got on his feet and started up the trail.

5

Near the top, the pass became a narrow ledge that ran up the face of the mountain at a forty-five degree angle. Footing was treacherous and the high winds that blew threatened at any moment to throw them off the edge of the cliff and down into the dark forest far below. It was nearing the end of the day. Behind the grey sky the unseen sun would be setting soon somewhere behind the western mountains at the other end of the valley. It had been a grey, cold day and soon it would be dark freezing night. Regvald looked up at the top of the pass and saw the entrance to a cave. Kelf saw it too.

"Is that its lair?" the farmer asked.

"Yes."

"Are we going in?"

"I am. You can remain outside or go back down to wait in the forest."

"It is too cold to wait outside," Kelf said, shrugging down

into his cloak. "And too far to go back. I will go with you."

Regvald limped forward. His ankle was now numb. The first half hour, walking on it had been agony. But as they'd gotten higher and the air colder, he felt the pain less and less. Now he could no longer feel anything in that leg from ankle to hip.

Together they trudged up the steep, rocky path to the cave entrance. They stood outside a moment. They listened, but no sounds came from inside.

As they entered, Kelf felt as though he were stepping into a big black mouth of some huge being that was about to swallow them. It was dark inside, but there was still enough daylight coming in through the entrance for them to see. It was an enormous cavern with a ceiling at least 100 feet high. The black walls curved up around them on either side, like the walls inside a gigantic stomach. The huge size of the cavern—just the size of the place—was intimidating. Kelf wondered if he had made a mistake. Maybe he should have waited down in the forest. This was really not in his line.

"This way," Regvald said. He moved further into the interior. Kelf followed closely on his heels. He kept the hilt of his new sword tight in the grip of his hand. As they proceeded further inside, Kelf saw a skull and several bones lying on the floor by the wall. His gaze turned away only to meet with another skull lying before the opposite wall.

Regvald continued further into the darkness. Kelf turned away from the skull and saw the hunter was getting ahead of him. He ran after him.

"Wait!" he whispered. "It's dark in here. It would be easy to get separated."

They went a few more feet.

"I don't think he's here," Kelf said. "The cavern seems empty. Maybe we should come back some other time."

"He'll be back," Regvald said. "When he does, we'll be here waiting."

"Yes, but-- " Kelf stepped to Regvald's side to reason with him and tripped over a pile of rocks. He lay there for a moment. The rocks were piled a good four feet high. He reached a hand out to get back to his feet, and his fingers touched something soft and cold.

"What's that!" He jumped to his feet. His eyes were used to the darkness now and he could see something sticking out of the rocks. It looked like a leg. But not a human leg. It was covered in cold, clammy skin that was not human.

"My God!" He fell to his knees and made the sign of the cross. He grabbed hold of one of the stones covering the body attached to the leg and threw it aside. Frantically, he removed more of the stones until he saw what lay beneath them.

"It's a baby dragon," the farmer said. "It's dead!"

He got to his feet and stepped back to look at the big mound of stones piled before him.

"It looks like there must be something else buried there," he said in a frightened whisper.

"Yes," Regvald said. "Another baby and their mother."

"What!" Kelf gaped at the hunter. "What do you mean? How do you know?"

"You asked me if I had ever slain a dragon before?" Regvald said. "The answer is yes. These three. They are the Black Mountain Dragon's wife and children. He must have buried them with these rocks."

"You! Killed them!"

"Yes."

Regvald's ankle was beginning to hurt again. He sat down on the floor of the cave.

"But why?" Kelf asked in shocked disbelief.

"I had to," the hunter said. "It was the only way."

"What are you talking about?"

"All right. I'll explain," Regvald said. "I was hunting this morning in the forest down below. Game was scarce, but my mind really wasn't on the hunt. I kept thinking about my sister and my niece. I've been thinking about them ever since the Dark Moon. And I thought about the Dark Mountain Dragon, and our arrangement with him. And that's when I decided it had to end. I came up here to try and kill the dragon. But he wasn't here. Instead I found he had a family. Two babies and a mate. The female heard me coming into the cavern and attacked. She was small by dragon standards. I killed her easily with my arrows and sword. And then I saw the babies in their nest and I knew I had to kill them too. Or else when they'd grown, they'd seek revenge. I killed them all. It's not something I'm proud of, but there was no other way. When it was over I hid there in that corner by the entrance and waited for the father to return to his lair."

Regvald's face suddenly darkened.

"He came back. He flew into the cavern and when he saw what had happened he let out a roar that nearly shattered my eardrums. He paced around the cave, and picked up the bodies of his children, one at a time, to see if there was some life left in them. When he was finally convinced that they were dead, he stood there and belched large sheets of flame from his nostrils. The cave lit up brighter than day, and I was afraid he would see me. I hesitated to attack. His size, the terrible ferocity of his rage. I was afraid. I knew my puny arrows would have no effect on him. I knew that if I shot even one arrow, I'd be dead soon thereafter. There was no use taking up my sword. At that moment, I knew terror. I was afraid for my life, and all my moral resolve to rid the world of evil fled me. I stood there quaking."

"I can't blame you," Kelf said.

"I said that most people are cowards," Regvald said. "And I am the worst coward of all. When the beast had his back to me I fled the cave and ran down the ledge and fairly sprinted down into the forest. I lay there in the woods shaking like a leaf in the wind. And that's when I discovered the terrible blunder I had made. I reached up for the medallion bearing my family emblem. I always wore it around my neck. It was gone. It must have fallen off in the cave.

"I knew the Black Mountain Dragon could trace its owner by the scent I left on it. As I lay there in the forest, I saw a dark shadow fly over, and I knew it was him and that he was heading for Hafnil. I ran down the mountain and through the forest as fast as I could. But I was too late."

He reached into the pocket of his jerkin and took out the amulet. "He put it in the wreckage of my home to let me know who had destroyed it."

He hefted the medallion and then with a hard flick of his wrist sent it sailing out through the cave entrance. "I will have no need for it after this day."

"What are you going to do?"

"What should I do, Kelf? Don't you see that I am responsible for the destruction of Hafnil, and all the dead. I tried to do what I thought was right. I thought it was better to make an accommodation with the devil than try to fight him. but instead, I unleashed Hell itself. I was wrong. Evil is too powerful. Unless you have the courage to go all the way."

"But you have no chance."

"Do you think I want one."

The way Regvald said that, Kelf knew there could be no further discussion.

"Get out of here while you can," the hunter said. "Go back to Hafnil. Tell the people there what happened. If I am successful, help them rebuild. If I fail, take everyone away. Take them to a place where there be no dragons, if such a place exists."

Kelf didn't want to leave. Regvald stood up and then they both heard the sound of flapping wings.

"God, no!" Kelf cried.

"Quick, in that corner," Regvald pointed to the spot by the entrance where he had hidden earlier. Kelf ran to it quickly and hid in the darkness.

From where he stood, Regvald could see a streak of orange behind the distant western mountain range. It was as if the sun wanted to take at least one peek at the world before this day ended. And then the Black Mountain Dragon appeared, and his massive body blotted out the dying sun. His wings were enormous, nearly spanning the wide entrance as it flew into the cavern. The dragon landed and his keen eyes saw Regvald immediately. He reared up on his legs and stood fully twenty feet high. Huge sheets of fire shot from his nose.

Regvald had his bow nocked and ready.

"Come, Dragon," he said. "No more accommodations. No more deals. It ends now."

His first arrow whizzed through the air and the Black Mountain Dragon whipped his long neck sideways to avoid it. Regvald fired another and this one caught the dragon in the center of the chest. The dragon came down on all fours and, extending his long snout, fired a wall of flame at Regvald. The hunter felt his breath taken away. He could feel the skin on his face and arms burning. He dived behind the mound of rocks that served as the dragon family's tomb and waited. The smell of his own burning flesh filled his nostrils. When the fire blast ended, he jumped up and fired more arrows. Feathered shafts protruded from the dragon's head, neck and breast. The dragon bellowed in rage. With an angry flap of its wings, it hopped up on top of the mound of rocks. Regvald fired more arrows, enraging the dragon even further. He threw away his bow, as the beast reared up on its hind legs. Drawing his sword, with a roar, he charged up the rock pile, and plunged his sword into the dragon's breast.

The Black Mountain Dragon flapped its wings and rose up and away from Regvald's blade. The hunter ran down the other side of the rock pile as the dragon landed on it and fired another sheet of flame at him. Regvald backed further away, backing closer to the black maw that lay outside the cave entrance. The beast dropped low and slithered across the rock pile toward him. Regvald backed further, bracing himself for the blast of fire that he expected to take the last breath from him. Out of the corner of his eye he saw Kelf still hiding in the dark shadows.

The dragon came closer. Its yellow eyes glared in rage at the puny man-thing that dared stand up to him. The sound of its breathing was so loud it seemed to echo around the walls of the cavern. Then, unexpectedly, Kelf jumped out of the shadows. He had the big water bag in his hands and he squeezed it. A jet of water shot out of the goatskin and splashed against the dragon's snout. The beast, surprised by the dousing, hesitated, its nostrils spurting smoke and water. Regvald charged in with a scream and plunged the point of his sword in between the dragon's two eyes. He ran up on its shoulder and scrambled onto its neck. Regvald locked his legs around the dragons' head and with two hands plunged his sword into the top of its cranium. The dragon flapped its wings frantically and came up from the ground in a short, feeble hop and then man and beast tumbled out through the cavern entrance.

Kelf ran to the edge and watched as the dragon, with Regvald still on its back, spun down the face of the mountvain, spinning like a broken kite. There was only silence as they fell, then a crash down far below.

6

Kelf stood there looking down for a long time. How long, he didn't know. But finally, he raised his eyes up and saw stars twinkling in the night sky. He looked over to the west and saw one or two lights from torches burning in the ruins of Hafnil. The survivors. They could start again. Rebuild. He could start again, as well. Plant new crops. Find a woman, start a family. He could have daughters and not have to live in fear of losing them. The Black Mountain Dragon was dead, thanks to Regvald.

What was it Regvald had said? "Who is to blame? He who commits evil, or he who strikes a bargain with it?"

He adjusted the sword hanging from his belt, and strode down the narrow ledge to the forest and the valley down below. He had much to tell the survivors of Hafnil.

THE HOSTAGE OF MALDON

The hostage began eagerly helping them;
he was of brave kin among the Northumbrians,
Ecglaf's son; Aesferth was name to him.
He flinched not at battle-play,. . .
ever and anon he inflicted some wound
while he could weapons wield.
    The Battle of Maldon
    ---An Anonymous Anglo Saxon Poet

1

In the Year of Our Lord 991, I, Aesferth, son of Ecglaf, was sent to the town of Maldon as hostage to Byrhtnoth, the Earl of Essex and leader of King Aethelred's Maldon militia. Relations between Maldon and my native Northumbria had been strained the last year. Not because of any hostile actions on my father's part, or because of any overt maneuvers by our army. No, the trouble in the little town on the other side of the Panta River was due mainly, I believe, to the treachery of one of Earldorman Byrhtnoth's close advisors, who had convinced the Earl that Maldon was in danger of an attack by my father's army. It was because of this treachery that I came to live in Maldon and eventually witnessed the inexplicable madness of what occurred there later that year.

I loathed having to serve under Byhrtnoth, as I would loathe serving any but my own Northumbrians. But being a good son, I had sworn to my father that I would obey the earldorman in all things for as long as it took to maintain the peace between our two peoples, or until ultimate hostilities broke out between us. In that event, I was determined I would return to my homeland to fight at my father's side.

My life in Maldon, where I was kept in the great house of Byrthnoth Manor where the Earl and his family lived, was one of monotonous boredom. There was little for me to do there. Being a man who craves excitement, I took it upon myself to become acquainted with some of the men in Byrhtnoth's small militia. It was a rag tag company, mostly of farmers and laborers, but some were men experienced in combat with sword, bow, and spear. I spent many an afternoon under the hazy Essex sun practicing swordsmanship with the likes of Wulfmaer, the earl's nephew, a man young in years, but possessed of a soul of a warrior, such as must have roamed the Earth in heroic days gone by.

One particular afternoon, as the steel in our hands clanged

loudly across the open field outside town where we were wont to practice, a thin man on a black steed stopped on the road that led back to town. I could feel the dark eyes of Godric, the Earl's chancellor and closest adviser, watching our every move. Of all the men in Maldon, he was the only one I had a disliking for. It was Godric who had convinced the Earl that Northumbria had evil intentions regarding Maldon.

I met the deep lunge and thrust of Wulfmaer's serpent-patterned blade with a stern parry. A sudden downturn of my sword threw Wulfmaer off balance. In a real fight, I would have had him at my mercy.

"Good ho!" the man on horseback shouted suddenly. "I believe you are dead, young Wulfmaer!"

"My opponent is a skilled swordsman," Wulfmaer rejoined, a smile on his face. "In his native land, he served his country well in several campaigns against barbarian tribes." His chestnut colored eyes glinted with a sudden hardness. "Would you care to try your hand, Godric? I'm sure Aesferth would be willing to oblige."

"Not today," the chancellor said. "I am on my way to meet with our good Earl, your uncle. And afterward I will lunch with his daughter, Aerlene and a few friends. But perhaps there will come a time."

At the mention of Byrhtnoth's daughter, the blood in my veins grew hot. "Still, Godric," I said, my pulse now throbbing inside my head, "a little sword play before lunch builds an appetite."

Godric smiled down at me. "Nay," he said. "I would not risk harming such a precious guest from Northumbria, even by accident." With fingers touching his forehead, he kicked the black stallion into a gallop and proceeded toward Maldon.

"Look how he rides the horse Byrhtnoth gave him," Wulfmaer said. "How is it my uncle cannot see that jackal for what he is?"

"I'd like to knock him down from that stallion," I said.

"And I know why," Wulfmaer said. "It's because of Aerlene.

I've seen the way you look at her. And she at you."

I felt a sensation of alarm. "You have?"

"Yes. And I'm not the only one. It's the talk of the hall."

My alarm was suddenly replaced with hot anger. "You and everyone else in Maldon would do well to pay mind to your own business and avoid intruding into the affairs of others."

"Ah," Wulfmaer said. "So it is an affair. What if my uncle hears of this?"

In exasperation I raised my sword and swung. "Come on, dog!" I shouted in mock anger. "See if I don't finish you this time."

With a gleeful shout, Wulfmaer raised his sword and parried my overbroad stroke and for the next few minutes, the two of us exorcised the animosity that Godric had raised in us in a strenuous fight that finally ended with the two opponents collapsing on the ground in breathless laughter.

2

Indeed, Wulfmaer was right. Life in Maldon would have been unbearable for me if it had not been for his friendship and the presence of Byrhtnoth's daughter, Aerlene. To call her beautiful does not do justice to her fair features and charming manner. Her crystal clear blue eyes, her golden hair that shone like corn silk in the sunlight, her heart-shaped face and full, red lips attracted me from the moment I first saw her.

The spark of love passed between us the second day of my arrival in Maldon, when I was presented to the family in the great hall of the earldorman's home. No words passed between us, but I knew somehow that she felt the same excitement when our eyes first met. Despite the awkwardness of my status in Maldon, I was determined from our first meeting that someday Aerlene would be mine.

But to dare to express anything openly was out of the question, especially after I learned that she was engaged to Godric, with a wedding planned for Christmas Day. Nevertheless, my heart would hear of no obstacles to achieving its desire and I was determined to meet with the Earl's daughter in private and express my feelings at first opportunity.

It had been months now since our first meeting, and I was desperate to arrange a private conversation with the object of my desire. However, life in Maldon afforded little privacy. But I learned that on certain mornings, Aerlene would ride one of her father's horses into the country. Wulfmaer's jibes now made it imperative that I act. Perhaps I was alone in my feelings, and only imagined the way she looked at me whenever we passed. I had to find out. I knew the trail she took and the morning after my conversation with Wulfmaer, I surreptitiously took a mount from the earldorman's stable and followed her.

I caught up to her in the deep woods to the west of town. At the sound of my mount's hooves she stopped and sat watching me as I approached. Wearing a light blue dress, her hair swept back with a yellow ribbon, she was a vision of loveliness.

"Aesferth," she said. Her voice speaking my name was like the sound of an angel singing. "Pray tell, what are you doing here?"

"Forgive me," I said, reining in my animal, and less successfully keeping control of my emotions. "I have wanted to see you, but in town there is no opportunity for private conversation. And what I have to tell you is very private. May we dismount?"

She hesitated, a slight frown, creasing her forehead.

"Very well." She dismounted as did I, and there under the eaves of one of the giant oaks that stand in the Maldon Forest, I told her everything. As I spoke, I searched her eyes for some response. I feared I would see laughter in those azure orbs, but as I went on, their expression changed from curiosity to intent interest. I had both her shoulders in my hands by the time I was finished pledging my eternal love and devotion. And now looking down into those eyes I saw a warm, glowing light arising. There was no derisive laughter, no protest or denial, and a sudden wave of emotion swept over me.

"I have waited long for you to speak so," Aerlene said at last.

"It is as you said, for me as well, from the very first."

I could no longer control the feelings bursting inside. I grabbed her closer and with her arms tight around me, I pressed my lips to hers. And there on the grass beneath the shady oak I, Aesferth of Northumbria, made Aerlene, daughter of Earl Byrhtnoth, my first and only love.

3

Aerlene sat up, brushing grass from her golden hair. "Well, my dear Northumbrian," she said with a pixyish smile, "what do you intend to do, now that you've stolen the honor of Godric's intended bride?"

"Tell me just one thing," I said. "Did you ever love Godric?"

She shook her head vehemently. "No. I despise him. I only agreed to marriage because my father wished it so. For father, there is no finer man in all the world than Godric. He bestows gifts and favors on the man as though he were his own son. Giving me to him was seen as only fitting in his eyes. So masterfully, has Godric taken control of my father's mind, these last two years. Through flattery, trickery, and false bravado, Godric has become the true source of power in Maldon."

"Even to the point of convincing Byrhtnoth that my father wishes him harm," I added. "I have observed Godric closely these last months, and I can only conclude that he has a plan to put your father in a position that will result in unseating him from his place of authority, so that he himself can become Earl of Maldon."

"I fear you may be right," Aerlene said. "I have tried to talk to father about Godric, but he will allow no evil to be spoken of the man he trusts above all others."

"No danger lurks for Maldon in Northumbria, I can assure you," I told her. "More peril comes from the Norsemen, who raid our Saxon cities with impunity. Your father should be more concerned with uniting Saxon towns against this foreign foe, than creating divisions that make us easier prey to the barbarians."

"You speak truly," Aerlene said. She looked up at me with imploring eyes. "But what are *we* to do, my new beloved?"

"I shall march into your father's hall and tell him we're in love and Godric's engagement is cancelled. Your father will agree to let us be married here in your church. If he will not give his consent, I will take you to Northumbria."

"I would be your bride anywhere in the world," Aerlene said. "But such precipitous action would bring only calamity. Indeed, the hostilities between our two domains that Godric has warned father about will surely come to pass."

"I care not for calamity."

"Let us be more circumspect," Aerlene said. "Let me tell Godric first that I have second thoughts on our wedding. Let me work on father and gradually let him accept my change of heart. When the time is right, we will both tell him what is in our hearts."

"I dislike delay," I protested.

But I could see Aerlene disliked the idea of breaking completely with her father and I thought of my pledge to my own father to serve as an honorable hostage. Finally I agreed that it might be wiser to take matters more slowly. I told her I would wait, but only one month. Little did I know that not a day would pass before Fate stepped forward to alter our lives forever.

4

Morning of the ninth of August it was. I, Earl Byrhtnoth, Godric, and several of the earldorman's retainers rode to the hunt in a field south of Maldon, where pheasants and quail were plentiful. The earl a tall, silver-haired man of sixty, rode his white stallion proudly at the head of our party. Godric, directly behind him, held out his gloved right arm, upon which was perched Black Shadow, his hunting falcon. I rode behind Godric, my mind and heart a swirl with the sudden developments of the day before. As I promised Aerlene, I said nothing about our new love to anyone, but just the sight of Godric sent the blood coursing up to my head.

I rode in uncharacteristic sullen silence.

Peasants ahead beat the grass in the field ahead of us, and suddenly a quail flew up into the sky. Godric lifted the leather hood from Black Shadow's head, allowed the bird to see its prey and with an upward movement of his arm, shouted: "Attack."

The falcon launched into the air and first flew high above the fleeing quail. The tiny bird seemed to sense its impending doom and let out a pathetic screech as it beat its wings frantically. Black Shadow now seemed to transform himself into an arrow shot from a bow as it dove for its prey. In seconds it was over.

While Godric waited for the falcon to return to his leather glove, a young man from town galloped across the field at breakneck speed.

"Sire," he said breathlessly, when he'd come abreast of us. "Norsemen! The Wolves of War have arrived!"

"Vikings!" Byrhtnoth said.

"Their ships are in the Panta, Sire," the boys said. "They've landed on Northey Island. At least 90 long ships. There are thousands of them, and they plan to raid Maldon this afternoon when the tide is out and they can cross the causeway."

Godric hooded Black Shadow and rode up next to Byrhtnoth. "What nonsense is this?"

"No nonsense, sir," the lad explained. "Maldon is in grave danger."

"And you say there are thousands of them?" Byrhtnoth asked.

"Aye."

"We have nothing to fear," Godric said. "Obviously another raiding party out for whatever loot they can plunder. Offer them some gold and jewels, they'll be on their way."

"Is that your solution, Godric?" I said, unable to stop myself. "Send them on their way, so they can rape and pillage somewhere else. Some place that isn't fortunate enough to possess enough tribute to satisfy them?"

The fire of anger blazed in Godric's eyes. "And are you, our dear guest from the north, now become the Earl's military adviser?"

"I offer no advice," I said. "Only a warning that it has been known for some time that Olaf Tryggvason and his northern wolves plan to move south this year. Maldon may be the last stand against the conquest of all England."

Godric started to fire back an answer, but Byrhtnoth raised an arm.

"Enough of this squabbling," he said. "Let us return to the city and see what those sea-faring dogs have in mind." Then to my surprise, the earl turned to me. "You may be right, Aesferth. If there is any chance we can destroy the Viking's fleet, we should take it before they invade further south. Godric, you will call up the levee, I want all my men behind me when I face Olaf."

Godric, seething inside, simply muttered, "Yes, sire."

5

It was a sight that sent cold chills down my spine. There on the other side of the Panta River, 90 some *drakkas*, as the wolves called their long dragon-ships, stood, anchored along the coast of Northey Island. On the far shore, tents were pitched where the Danes had made their camp. Viking men stood along the shoreline, taunting insults and threats across the river.

A narrow wooden bridge ran from the Maldon shore to the island. But there had been much rain lately and the tides ran high. Except at lowest of low tide, the bridge was underwater, and impassible. Olaf said he and his men would cross later today when the waters ebbed.

Byrthnoth, now in full armor and looking every inch the leader of Aethelred's militia, rode his horse up to the river bank near the bridge. Behind him on foot came the mere 1,000 men that made up his army. The scarcely-trained farmers and laborers carried newly issued weapons gingerly, as if they only half-knew how to use them. Leading them on horseback, were the other aristocrats of Maldon, men with some military experience, including Godric. I walked in the ranks next to Wulfmaer, and two others of the warrior class, Aelfhere and Maccus.

Except for the horses the noblemen rode, there were none left in Maldon. Before meeting with Olaf Tryggvason, Earl Byrthnoth ordered everyone to send their horses away into field and forest. The Earl had already determined there would be no retreat or surrender. Now he and his officers stood facing the Wolf Fleet moored across the water.

From a tent pitched close to the river bank emerged a huge man dressed in armor. Long red hair and beard streamed down over the chain mail that covered his massive chest. He came to the water's edge, and stood with his legs widespread, massive fists resting on his hips.

"I am Olaf Tryggvason," the Norseman shouted. "Whom do I address?"

The Earl identified himself.

"I give you one chance," Olaf shouted back. "Give us tribute or have harsh war. There is no need for us to destroy each other, if you are rich enough to pay. Confirm a truce with your gold. If you are the highest here, decide that you will ransom your people and in return receive peace from us. We will return to the sea."

Byrhtnoth looked back along the ranks behind him and turned again to Olaf. "Do you see our Saxon people ready to defend their homes? They will give you spears for tribute, poisoned point, and old sword. Here stands an undisgraced earl who will defend this country, my lord Aethelred's folk and homeland."

The Dane stood silent for a moment, his hands still on his hips, then suddenly rumbling laughter rolled across the river toward us. "Then war it is," he shouted.

At a signal from the Earl, we in the ranks all stepped forward and lined the river bank, armed with our swords, spears, bows, and bucklers. Olaf raised his hairy arm and from tents, and long boats poured hords of Norsemen, waving axes and swords. They lined the opposite shore in a force at least three or four times the size of our thousand men. Yet we of the Earl's militia—yes, in the excitement of impending battle, I now considered myself such—

stood silently, but determined and ready to fight.

But with the tide still too high, there was little either side could do, except throw taunts, and send arrows wildly across the river. It would be later that afternoon when the tide would be low enough for the Vikings to cross the wooden bridge that the attack would begin.

After the initial challenge and threats subsided, Olaf returned to his tent, and Earl Byrhtnoth dismounted his white stallion and began to place his men at their stations, and showed them how to hold their weapons and shields firm in their hands and how they should stand and hold their places. I stood in the front of the ranks with Wulfmaer, Aelfhere and Maccus, where we with some fighting expertise could encourage and instruct some of those who had never fought before.

I waited for the beginning of battle, but my thoughts were only of Aerlene, whom Byrhtnoth had placed under the protection of guards in the upper tower of the manor house. Inwardly, I grieved that my sudden happiness should suddenly be dashed by this dire turn of events. Looking across the water at the dragon-headed ships floating in the river, they truly seemed not human, but demons sent from the netherworld. I wondered if I would ever see Aerlene again.

6

Soon the tide lowered. Byrhtnoth ordered Wulfstan, a war-hardened warrior to hold the bridge. Wulfstan took Aelfhere and Maccus with him. Wulfmaer and I stepped forward to join them, but the fierce Wulfstan told us to wait. Our time would come later. We, and all the others, watched as the three valiant men went out to the middle of the one-man wide bridge and met the oncoming charge of screaming wolf-warriors. Wulfstan in grim silence, lashed out with his sword. Steel rang and flashed and the first Viking invader at first seemed repelled by the Saxon defender's ferocity. But he soon roused himself and his blade became a blur of reflected sunlight. Yet Wulfstan gave not an inch, and a moment later the burly Norseman pitched over the bridge railing, a bloody hole torn through his chest mail. On came more of them. Wulfstan fought like a man possessed, sending two more of the pagan seamen to their deaths.

Aelfhere and Maccus took turns in the lead, spelling Wulfstan when he drew a wound to his shoulder. My two new friends fought as valiantly as Wulfstan and half a dozen more wolf-warriors plunged into the river. Now archers gathered on at the base of the bridge on our side of the river, and began showering the Norsemen with arrows, as they stepped onto the causeway. The northern devils soon lost their desire to board the wooden planks of the bridge, and Wulfstan, fighting again with his companions cleared the bridge of the Vikings who had gotten that far.

"Come, devils," Wulfstan shouted at the far bank. "We're waiting for you."

In this pause of the fighting, the earl came along the ranks and stopped in front of me. "Aesferth," he said. "What is our hostage doing here? This is not your fight. I would not have you injured or killed while you serve as your father's guarantor of peace between our nations. I release you of your obligation. Go now, back to Northumbria, while you still can."

"Sire, you do me dishonor," I said. "I will stand and fight here in Maldon as if it were my own home."

"But why?"

At that moment Godric rode up on his horse, Black Shadow resting on his arm.

"I fight to protect Maldon because in it lives the one person who means more to me than life itself," I said, glancing up defiantly at Godric.

"What's this?" the earl asked perplexed. "What do you mean?"

"I've suspected the young hostage has taken a fancy to my betrothed for some time now, Sire," Godric said. "But this is not the time to discuss such matters." He looked back anxiously to the other side of the river. "Sire, it is not too late to empty our treasury and give these monsters what they've come for. With no loss of life, we shall be rid of them overnight."

"A coward's solution," I snarled. "We must make our stand here. All of England depends on it."

"Silence, young hostage," the earl said. He gave Godric a stern look. "I agree with Aesferth, Godric," he said. "You disappoint me, chancellor. There is more at stake here than our lives. There will be no tribute paid."

Then a Viking horn sounded across the river. Olaf Tryggvason stood now at the water's edge.

The Earl's white-maned head turned toward the river. "I must go now."

"Let me go with you," I said. "I would fight by your side if you will."

"And I, uncle," Wulfmaer piped in. "A nephew should be at his uncle's side at a time like this."

"Very well," the earl said. "Come with me, the both of you. With young men of such fighting spirit, I feel the more strongly we shall defeat our foe."

With Godric, Wulfmaer and the earl I rode to the edge of the river where Byrhtnoth answered Olaf the Viking's call.

"Have you called to surrender?" the earl shouted.

Then something transpired the like of which I have never witnessed or heard of before or since.

"We cannot pass your bridge, Earldorman," Olaf said. "Your defenders are too stalwart. If you are as brave a people in your deeds as you are in words, let us cross the bridge and lead our forces across the water. Let us land on your shore and we shall fight—a battle such as no man has ever seen. Let the fates decide who will live and who will die. Who will conquer and be conquered."

I stood next to Byrhtnoth as he gathered his advisers around him, and heard their conversation. The Earl said he was of a mind to let the Vikings cross.

"This is madness," Godric said. "First you refuse to pay tribute, and now you want to let them on our shore? We have only to hold the bridge and wait. They will tire of this situation, and will leave. Refuse their request."

"And when they leave here, where do they go?" the earl asked. "To another city less able to defend itself, from where they will launch further incursions? No, this is the moment. If we let them cross, we may be able to defeat them once and for all. Sheer count of numbers is against us, I admit, but we must try to stop them."

7

And so it came to pass, that the Maldon levee stood ready and watched as nearly 4,000 Vikings crossed the causeway and lined up on the river bank. The Earl had pulled his forces back into the marshy land that fronted the Panta River. As I watched the staggering number of invaders taking their battle places, I feared that, noble and valiant as Byrhtnoth's motives were, he had made a terrible miscalculation. The day could only end in disaster for us. I thought of Aerlene back at the manor and felt sheer terror at the thought of what would become of her at the hands of these pagan devils, after they had killed us.

As the Vikings formed their ranks, the Earl ordered his men to form a war-hedge. The troops linked their shields together, forming a solid wall of defense. The Earl, Godric and several officers on horseback, along with Wulfmaer and I on foot, traversed to the far end of the shield wall. Olaf Tryggvason now stood at the front of his men and looked from one end of our war-hedge to the other and at the ranks of swordsmen and archers behind them. Then loudly shouting the name of Wodan, their God of War, he raised his sword arm and began the charge. Godric lifted the hood from Black Shadow's head and the bird flew toward the Norseman as Byrhtnoth raised his arm and ordered the men forward.

Arrows flew towards us, the poisoned arrowheads tearing into the leather covered wood of our shields. As the war-hedge advanced, the Earl, Godric and the rest of us fell in behind it, followed by men ten ranks deep. As we moved closer to the barbarians, I could hear first the arrowheads digging into the bucklers and bouncing off their iron-framed edges. Then in a roar that was deafening, armored Norse bodies crashed against the shields, and I heard the chop of axes and the ring and slash of swords cutting the defense wall to pieces. In a moment the snarling, savage faces of our foes came toward us.

The Earl charged ahead on his white stallion, his gold-hilted sword in the air, followed closely by his small cadre of officers. Godric, it seemed, hung a bit behind. But I was too busy to pay much notice. A lumbering giant of a man with an axe came charging toward me. He raised his battle axe high over his head, his grey eyes wide and wild in battle lust. I stood my ground and waited until the axe blade started its downward swing. I took one short step back, almost into the point of the spear of the man behind me, and the blade whooshed downward an inch from my chest. With both hands on the hilt of my long sword I swung and saw blood spurt as the man's wrist separated from his arm. In rage and pain, he screamed and tried to take his sword from his belt with his remaining hand. Before he could loosen the blade from its scabbard, I thrust the tip of my weapon through the iron ringlets that covered his chest.

I don't remember even seeing the Viking fall, for that moment two more of the monsters were on me. In such close quarters, there is no time for tactics or calculation. If one wants to survive battle with berserkers, one must oneself become berserker. And with a madness and ferocity I had never known myself capable of, I began to slash, stab, and hack at any thing that came close to me. Screaming bloody curses made of words I had never used before, I moved into the swirling madness of blood and flying limbs.

My hands felt the crack and crush of bone and sinew through the handle of my sword. My ears were deafened by the roaring screams of savage men on both sides. My nostrils quivered at the coppery smell of blood everywhere. My eyes were blinded by a red curtain of madness and rage, so that all I saw was a blur of weapons, shields, and falling men.

Then a cry of anguish went up from our side. I shook my head to clear my eyes and saw the Earl, still on his white steed, in the center of the battle, but with a Viking spear protruding from his abdomen. The Vikings closed in and Byrhtnoth's horse was pushed down, the Earl tumbled out of his saddle and sat on the ground. Without a word, Wulfmaer and I pushed through to the Earl and fought back his nearest attackers.

Wulfstan appeared, and while that fierce warrior and I held the pagans at bay, Wulfmaer leaned over the Earl. "Take this spear from me, nephew," he said. Wulfmaer lay his sword down and pulled the point of the spear from his uncle, then looked about, and with a snarl on his face, he hurled it. It caught one of the berserkers in the neck and the man fell back amidst his confederates. I saw Byrhtnoth standing now, holding his sword in one hand, his other arm around Wulfmaer's shoulders. The tide of battle had pushed me further away from them. I tried to get closer, but too many men, adversary and friend alike blocked my way. I saw Wulfmaer, his uncle, and Wulfstan surrounded by twenty of the demon warriors, who closed in on them like a pack of rabid wolves.

Although Aethelred's brave, if not foolish, thane had fallen, still the men of Maldon did not run. They stayed and fought as only men who have everything to lose can fight. Until that is, they beheld a sight that totally unnerved even the best of them. They saw a figure on a white steed galloping away from the battle, through the marshlands, headed for the safety of the manor.

"Byrhtnoth retreats!" some of them cried. "The earl leaves us!"

But it was not the earl who had ridden off. The earl lay dead under a pile of bodies. I had seen who had jumped into Byrhtnoth's empty saddle. I had seen Godric, in mad panic, commandeer the earl's mount and force the stallion to trample all who got in his way, so he could escape the battle. He must have been dislodged from his own black steed, as had the Earl. But somehow he escaped any wounds and found his way to the earl's horse. Again, the desperation of my own situation precluded any attempt to stop him. All I could do was watch him, Black Shadow winging high in the sky over him, as he rode back to the manor. To Aerlene.

I had begun to tire from all the fighting, but the thought of Godric riding to Aerlene brought me back to life instantly. My sword arm seemed suddenly strengthened, and with renewed vigor my steel-edged blade tore into all from the North who stepped in my way. To my rear, I saw the black head of Godric's black steed rising and falling as the beast screamed and reared on its hind legs amidst the boiling chaos of the battle. Some of the men of Maldon now sought to retreat as they thought their leader had done. Others retained their resolve and fought on. Through this swirling tumult, I fought my way to Godric's animal, hacking through the twisting, roiling sea of fighters, until at last I grabbed hold the horse's reins and swung up on its back. I kicked the horse's ribs mercilessly, forcing him to push through the mob.

I knew the battle of Maldon was lost, and my only thought now was to get back to Byrhtnoth Manor and find Aerlene before the Vikings arrived. If Godric be there, I muttered to myself, God help him. For the cowardice and treachery he had shown this day, I could forgive him. Not all men are made for battle. But if he had intentions of forcing his way on the woman I loved and carrying her off, I would kill him.

8

The peace and quiet of the manor with its well-manicured lawns and shrubbery, the doves cooing in the high rafters, the ivy climbing up the walls of the tower now seemed unreal as a dream, when I rode through the gate up to the front entrance. It was a dream, I knew, that soon would become a nightmare as the brutish hordes from the North Sea moved inland and began their pillage and rape.

The Earl's white stallion, now with red stains on its sweat-shiny coat, stood in front of the main building, panting in exhaustion, as I jumped from Godric's horse. I bounded up the front steps and entered the main hall. Kendrick, one of the manor guards left to protect Aerlene stood blocking my way. He was dressed in chain mail and helmet.

"I'm sorry," he said, his hand on the hilt of his sword. "Chancellor Godric has instructed me to allow no one entrance."

I kept moving quickly toward him. He seemed to be the only one on guard. The others must have already run away. "Out of my way, Kendrick." His sword started to come out of its scabbard. With a rush that caught him by surprise, I leaped at him, held his sword hand down on the scabbard, and sent my fist crashing into his face. His nose shattered under my knuckles and I hit him once more, as he fell to the mahogany floor. I jumped over his senseless body and ran for the entrance to the tower.

An archway on the side of the hall led me down a narrow corridor to a door. Wooden steps ran straight upward twenty feet in darkness. I clamored upward blindly, drawing my sword. Halfway up the stairs, I heard something hurtling through the air, then, a screeching, taloned fury struck me full in the face. Godric had sent Black Shadow to meet me. Blinded by darkness, I felt but could not see the feathery menace as it repeatedly dove at my head. I covered my eyes with one hand, but already I felt hot blood dripping down my forehead and cheeks, and I could taste it in my mouth. I sent my sword out, flailing wildly in the air around me, all the while moving relentlessly upward step by step. Finally I could see daylight coming from a door at the top of the tower. A man's silhouette appeared in the doorway. Godric. At that moment, Black Shadow flew in front of me, clearly outlined against the light from the door. I swung my sword and the devilish avian was rent in two, feathers flying everywhere.

With a mad yell, I charged up the stairs. With a shouted

curse, Godric ran down to meet me. He knew if he met me on the stairs, rather than at the top of the tower, he would have the advantage of the higher position. Our blades cracked loudly against each other, and sparks lit the darkness of the stairwell.

"Maldon has no need of hostages now," Godric hissed, as our swords momentarily locked together. "And what good is a dead hostage anyway?"

"When you fled the river," I snapped back, "you broke the resolve of the militia. If there had been any chance at all for victory, you snatched it from your dead earl's grasp. And now you would steal his daughter. It is you who will die."

Godric pushed me back and again and again swung his sword down at my head. With each shower of sparks I could see the madness in the chancellor's face. The lust for battle that had eluded him on the banks of the Panta now possessed him with the intensity of a demon. The best I could do was parry each attack, and send short jabbing stabs at his knees, legs and lower torso. Backwards down the stairs he pushed me, and my only recourse was to maintain a defensive posture, until Fate might see fit to give me an opportunity to strike. And that day Fate was kind.

When we backed down to the step upon which I had slain Black Shadow, Godric's foot slipped on the pile of blood and feathers that had been his pet falcon. His leg shot out from under him and he crashed down on his back, his armor splintering the wood of the steps. With a yell I jumped up on the step and before he could swing his blade at my midsection I sent the tip of my weapon deep through his chest. I heard steel sheering through steel and then the crunch of blade against breast bone. There was a soft gasp, and then Godric was no more.

I jumped over his body and rushed up the stairs to the room at the top. From the doorway, I saw Aerlene standing by the narrow window in the tower wall, her pale blue eyes wide with fear. For a moment she stood in disbelief, then a faint smile came to her lips. "Aesfertth!" She ran to me. I threw my sword down and took hold of her. Never had an embrace ever meant so much. Never had a kiss ever brought such happiness to two lovers.

"Maldon is lost," I finally told her when our emotions had subsided a bit.

"Father?" she asked.

"His brave heroism today in the face of such terrifying odds will be long remembered in song and story," I told her.

But there was no time for delay. It would not be long before the first of the Northern barbarians swept over the manor. We would have time only to take what was on our backs, find fresh horses in the Earl's stable and flee the manor. Two days ride by back roads would bring us to Northumbria, where my father would welcome his returned hostage and his new bride-to-be.

The world had turned suddenly. We could see smoke coming from the waterfront. The old world was burning behind us as we rode away from the manor. In a few decades all of England would be under the rule of Vikings, and all that had happened in Maldon would be for naught. But still, saddened as we were by the loss we had just suffered, at that moment we rode together with hearts full of hope.

ABOUT THE AUTHOR

John M. Whalen

John M. Whalen is a former Washington, D.C., reporter, who currently is the author of books of speculative fictiion. His works include sword and sorcery stories, space westerns, and fantasy. He also writes movie reviews for Cinemaretro.com.

PRAISE FOR AUTHOR

John M. Whalen's new novel TRAGON OF RAMURA is a sword-and-sorcery adventure in the classic mold. . . I'm naming it an honorary Front Porch Book and recommending it if you're a fan of sword and sorcery action.

- JAMES REASONER'S REVIEW ON ROUGH EDGES.

Vampire Siege at Rio Muerto:

. . .an interesting plot with plenty of twists and action to keep your attention, and Mordecai Slate works as a protagonist. . .flashes of brilliance in the prose."

- BLACKGATE MAGAZINE

"The Big Shutdown" by John M. Whalen takes fandom back to its roots with raw action and a comforting sense of direction. With a fast paced collection of harsh adventures in the guise of the old west, but with the flair and unpredictability of a space drama, readers are in for a rootin' tootin' fun ride. . . . a fun read that will remind readers just why pulp fiction, westerns, and ray guns belong together.

- AMAZING STORIES MAGAZINE

BOOKS BY THIS AUTHOR

Tragon Of Ramura

A dream starts Tragon of Ramura and his friend/bodyguard Yusef Ahmed on a search for an amulet said to be the source of the most powerful magic in the universe, Their search leads them to the lost city of Caiphar and the beautiful and mysterious Sai-Ul-San, high priestess of the cult of Zoth-Amin. Tragon finds the Crimson Eye of Caiphar, but the city holds dark secrets of an evil a thousand years old that threaten to unleash a demon intent on destroying the world. Can Tragon defeat the ancient forces that rule Caiphar, or will he remain trapped forever in the Tower of Lost Souls?

Vampire Siege At Rio Muerto

A wealthy New Mexican ranchero hires Monster Hunter Mordecai Slate to track down the vampire who ravished his daughter. Don Pedro Sanchez wants Slate to bring him back alive, so he can have the pleasure of driving in the stake himself. Slate travels from Socorro to Las Cruces where he finds his prey, Kord Manion, and comes up with an unusual way to transport him back north. Kord's brother, Dax, and his gang of vampire outlaws follow in pursuit, half a day behind. During the chase, Slate stops to rescue a girl in trouble and tries to get her out of harm's way. His journey leads him to a desert ghost town called Rio Muerto, where he will face his greatest challenge in the ultimate battle between good and evil.

The Big Shutdown

Space Western Action. Across the desolate planet Tulon moves a solitary figure. Jack Brand, former officer in the Tulon Security Force, is on a search. Seven years ago, he led a tactical squad that included his sister, Terry, into a deadly ambush in the desert. The Wilkersons, a Nomad gang who robbed a Trans-Exxon payroll, wiped out four members of his unit, kidnapped Terry, and left Brand for dead. Brand recovered from his wounds, and swore he would never leave Tulon until he found his sister. But time is running out. The energy conglomerates that own Tulon are shutting the oil rich planet down. New fuel sources have made oil obsolete. Soon the last ships will leave for Earth. Over the course of his search, Brand travels from desert wasteland to steaming jungles, from a city at the bottom of the sea to a desert town run by alien gangsters. Along the way, Brand meets a gallery of exotic characters, finds the love of his life, and survives the barbaric planet through quick wit, fast reflexes, and the Electro-Pistol holstered to his hip. It's epic space opera like no other.

This Ray Gun For Hire

Who is Frank Carson? A paid assassin? A killer for hire? Or just a tough trouble shooter for rent? Hero or villain? You decide. Some say he's the kind of guy you call for a job so dirty or so dangerous nobody else will touch it. He knows danger and what can happen to people in the noir world of Tulon in the 22nd Century. There's nobody tougher or smarter. Frank Carson. John M. Whalen's THIS RAY GUN FOR HIRE . . . AND OTHER TALES.